Love Runs Deep

The Coleman Series

Katie Winters

Chapter One

September 1992

Charlie Coleman had always adored his father. But in the years since he'd entered high school, he'd noticed their relationship had changed, at first in marginal and unimportant ways and then in ways that left Charlie fuming about once or twice a year. His mother, Estelle, whom Charlie loved, always consoled him, saying that Charlie and Roland were "two peas in a pod" and "more alike than Charlie could fully understand." This wasn't what Charlie wanted to hear, especially immediately after Roland had shown such anger toward him— but Charlie wouldn't have dreamed of saying his mother was wrong. It wasn't in his nature.

Charlie was a senior in high school. In many respects, everything in his life was perfect. He was popular, good-looking, the captain of the football team, and an A-student— and his girlfriend was none other than Shawna Davies, who everyone knew was the most beautiful girl in school. Unlike traditional football players' girlfriends, most of whom were cheerleaders, Shawna was an academic. She always had her head in a book, took advanced math and science classes, and loved having intellectual discussions with Charlie that frequently kept them awake deep into the night. When Charlie and Shawna hung out with their friends and talked like this, their friends suggested they were growing up way too soon and that they should just chill out and enjoy Nantucket like the rest of them. But Charlie relished those conversations. Sometimes, when it was just him and Shawna together, he felt like they were the only two people in the world.

It was a Friday in September, one of those blue-skied days that reminded you of the glories of summer vacation but with a bite to the air that required a jacket and maybe a mug of hot cider. Charlie walked Shawna home from school, kissing her on the front porch of her family's home until she swatted him away playfully. "Good luck tonight," she said.

"I don't need luck," Charlie replied, pretending to be cocky.

"You're such an arrogant jock! I don't know why I'm involved with you."

"Come on. You like being with the captain of the football team," Charlie joked.

"I'd prefer it if you were the captain of the bowling team. But football is okay, I guess." She shrugged her shoulders to add a flair of drama.

Charlie floated home, exhilarated with his love for Shawna and his excitement for the football game that evening against Oak Bluffs High School, which was located on Martha's Vineyard. He was needed at the football field at five that afternoon, and he planned to stop by the Coleman House to eat a sandwich, say hello to his mother, grab his cleats, and then hit the road.

Back at home, Charlie's father, Roland, hovered over the kitchen counter, gazing down at blueprints for a new project he planned to build on the coast. Unlike Roland's father before him, who'd worked in trading, Roland had gone out on his own to create a very successful business that designed and developed hotels and luxury homes on Nantucket, Martha's Vineyard, and other islands in the area. It had made him very wealthy, a fact that everyone on Nantucket Island knew well and respected him for, including Charlie.

"Hi, Dad." Charlie filled a glass of water in the kitchen sink and eyed his father's blueprint, which he couldn't make sense of.

Roland seemed to be in one of his moods. He didn't take his eyes off the blueprint and instead grunted hello. Charlie placed his water on the counter and began to make himself a sandwich, deciding that it was better to get away from Roland during this mood rather than wait for him to explode. Charlie had made that mistake before.

But as Charlie spread mayonnaise on a piece of bread, Roland adjusted the blueprint in a way that brought his elbow further to the right than Charlie had anticipated. Suddenly, it smashed against the glass of water, and the water sloshed along the edge of the blueprint and began to creep toward the middle. Charlie stared at the scene in horror, his mayonnaise knife lifted.

"What the heck did you do?" Roland cried, pulling the blueprint off the counter so fast that the water droplets splashed across the floor.

Charlie stuttered, wanting to point out that he hadn't

been the one to spill the water. But when Roland was in one of his moods, there was no standing up for yourself. Not in his house.

"You think you're a big man, don't you?" Roland continued. "You think you can just swagger around my house and make a mess of my blueprints? Do you realize how important these are?"

Charlie's nostrils flared. He shoved the mayonnaise back in the fridge angrily and suddenly heard himself say, "You don't have to act like such a bully."

Roland's eyes narrowed into slits as Charlie glowered at him and walked out of the kitchen and up the staircase, past both his sisters' bedrooms and into his. In Hilary's bedroom, she listened to an album loudly on her boombox while Samantha's room remained quiet. He wouldn't have been surprised if Samantha wasn't around at all. She spent a great deal of her time at their Great Aunt Jessabelle's place, mostly because she didn't get along with their father at all, especially not since Roland had suggested her desire to pursue a social work degree went against the Coleman family values. When Samantha had complained to Charlie about this, Charlie had said, *"I don't know. Maybe you should just try to make Dad happy? He does so much for this family."* And Samantha hadn't spoken to him for a week, which had devastated Charlie so much that he'd apologized to her.

Just before Charlie disappeared into his bedroom, however, Samantha's door opened, and she smiled out from behind a curtain of her blond hair. "Hey."

"Hey." Charlie shifted his weight, unsure of what to say. He was still reeling from the incident downstairs.

"What happened in the kitchen?" Samantha asked.

Charlie grimaced. "Nothing."

"I heard Dad's voice," Samantha pushed. "He sounded really angry."

"He's just working," Charlie said, not wanting to feed Samantha's dislike of their father, which upset him a great deal.

Charlie stepped into his bedroom, but he wasn't able to close the door quickly enough to keep Samantha out. There she was, standing in the doorway with a look on her face that suggested she wanted to have a serious talk.

"He flies off the handle so quickly sometimes," Samantha said.

Charlie shrugged. "I can't really think about it. I have a game tonight."

"I just don't think he should get away with treating us like that," Samantha said.

Charlie sat on the edge of his bed, not wanting to get into this.

"Have you ever wondered why Dad doesn't talk to his father?" Samantha asked.

"No," Charlie lied, for, in fact, his father's lack of relationship with his own father terrified him. He never wanted to live in a world where Roland stopped talking to him or vice versa. He was willing to set aside every difference, every cruel word. And in fact, he was already starting to regret what he'd said downstairs— and had made up his mind to return to Roland and tell him he shouldn't have said what he said.

"Really?" Samantha demanded.

"I'm sure Dad has his reasons," Charlie said.

Samantha sighed. "You're lucky, you know. You're the golden child of this family. I'm the black sheep."

"You are not," Charlie said. "Mom and Dad love you. Hilary and I love you."

"But they won't let me do what I want to do."

"You said yourself that you're already going to do what you want, regardless of what they say," Charlie reminded her.

Samantha kicked her foot out in front of her. "I just wish I had his support. It's stupid, I know."

"It's not." Charlie palmed the back of his neck, unsure of what to say. He was suddenly completely overwhelmed by the idea that Roland wouldn't want to have a relationship with him anymore. "I have to get out of here soon. You coming to the game?"

"I'll be there," Samantha told him. "You're the only person on earth who would make me sit through an entire football game."

"Funny. Shawna said the same thing," Charlie said with a smile.

Downstairs, Charlie hunted for his father to apologize, but Roland had taken his blueprints with him, gotten into his truck, and sped off. This chilled Charlie to the bone. But before he could dwell on it for too long, the phone rang with a call from Marcus, Charlie's best friend.

"Hey, man!" Marcus was bright and cheery, such a contrast to how Charlie currently felt. "Got some bad news. My car just died out on me."

"Shoot." Charlie searched through the fridge again for ingredients to make himself a last-minute sandwich. "Want me to pick you up on the way?"

"That would be great," Marcus replied. "Mind taking me to the party tonight?"

"Charlie's taxi, at your service."

"Man, you're a lifesaver." After a pause, he said, "Is there something wrong?"

"Naw. Nothing wrong." Marcus had always had an eerie understanding of what was going on in Charlie's mind. "I'll see you soon, okay?"

"Cool," Marcus said. "See you."

Charlie ate his sandwich, a few pretzels and carrot sticks, then grabbed his cleats and ran out the door. The drive to Marcus' place took no more than five minutes, and when he pulled into the driveway, Marcus stormed out of the front door with a big, excited grin on his face. Although Charlie knew they both looked a lot different than they did when they'd met at the age of five— in kindergarten, no less— Marcus' grin seemed just the same as ever. Although the rules of their lives had changed, they were still just kids exploring the world around them.

The game against Oak Bluffs High started at seven-thirty that night. At seven twenty-five, the Nantucket team was dressed and cleated, their helmets attached securely, huddled together to listen to Charlie give them final words of encouragement and excitement. Charlie raised his fist and gave a speech, one about teamwork, the love they had for Nantucket, and the fact that, because he was a senior, now, every game counted more than ever before. Afterward, they ran in place, smashing their cleats against the locker room floor so that the sound echoed along the lockers and made them shake. Once, Shawna had heard this from down the hall and called them "animals."

Out on the field, Charlie got into position as, in the stands, hundreds of Nantucket and Martha's Vineyard residents gathered, eating popcorn, speaking loudly as the night lights began to glow on their faces, taking over as night filled the sky. Charlie stole a glance at where his family normally sat and found only Estelle, Samantha, and Hilary there without Roland. His stomach tightened with an uneasy feeling. Was Roland going to hold on to this grudge for long? Could Roland ever convince his father these silly arguments weren't worth holding onto anger?

But before Charlie could dwell on Roland any longer, the referee blew his whistle, and they were off to the races on the game. Charlie allowed his captain role to take over as he threw the football forward, frequently into Marcus' hands as Marcus ran with ease, his long legs stretching him into one, then two, and then three touchdowns. The crowd howled with excitement, knowing that they were witnessing something very special. Never had Charlie felt that he and Marcus had more power. Never had he felt such magic on the field.

The game raged on for nearly three hours. Charlie felt capable and strong, always keeping their score about ten or twelve above Oak Bluffs'. In the last thirty seconds, just for the heck of it, he blasted the football far down the field and watched as Marcus made an incredible catch— one that seemed miraculous, given how far away Marcus had been from where he caught it when Charlie had first thrown it. As the clock counted down to zero, the crowd howled, chanting Marcus' name, and Charlie hurried to his best friend, threw his arms around him, and leaped up and down with the rest of the team.

In this moment of impossible joy and success, Charlie hardly thought of his father or his future or anything besides being seventeen and on top of the world. He knew he was one of the luckiest people in the world— and he felt sure that his luck would go on forever.

Chapter Two

Nora was sixty-seven years old with a bank account that reminded her frequently that she could never retire. She still lived at the old Victorian home she and her ex-husband had bought right after the birth of their son so many years ago, and although she could have gotten a great deal of money in its sale, Nora refused to give it up, saying it was the last link she had to the past. Most people understood this, even if it was irrational. People understood the importance of memories, above all.

It was morning in early July, not long after the Fourth of July celebrations, and Nora woke at seven, just as she always did, and made herself a bowl of oatmeal and fruit. As she ate, she listened to a podcast about the history of Nantucket, which told in-depth stories about people who'd lived and died on the island many years ago. It made her feel like a part of the greater tapestry of all the eras of Nantucket history. Because she didn't have many friends, the voice on the podcast had begun to feel like one.

Nora showered and dressed in a simple red dress and a little hat, then set out on her daily walk to the store she owned and operated in downtown Nantucket. There, she sold paintings and ceramics from local artists, turning a profit that kept both her and the artists alive. The store itself was cute and drenched with light, and tourists streamed in and out all through the spring, summer, and fall, grateful to take a piece of Nantucket creativity back with them. Nora enjoyed meeting so many people from all over the world, talking to them about their vacations, their children, their careers, and what they missed most from back home. A woman from Michigan said that she missed her dog so much that she wanted to end her vacation early to go back to him. "Why not bring him with you next time?" Nora had suggested. "Nantucket loves dogs."

For lunch, Nora met her only sister, Cecilia, at a downtown lunch spot, where they ate sandwiches and chatted about easy things, like the weather and recent recipes they'd tried. Always when Cecilia spoke of her daughter and her husband, Nora's soul curled up into a ball of sorrow, but Nora did her best to ask all the right questions and listen intently. It wasn't Cecilia's fault that Nora's life had fallen apart. It wasn't Cecilia's fault that she remained happy while Nora was alone in the world.

It was only when Cecilia spoke of her grandson, Jax, that Nora brightened. Jax was twenty-one and extremely intelligent and kind, with a wicked sense of humor that left Nora bent over with laughter. Jax had tried out college for a year or two but then had returned to the island, saying he missed it too much. Since then, he'd taken college classes online and worked jobs at restaurants throughout Nantucket, both in the kitchen and as a server. Now that he was twenty-one, he talked romantically about becoming a bartender, which worried Cecilia to death. Nora could understand his desire, though. There was something about being twenty-one and out in the vibrant bar scene, chatting to locals and tourists deep into the night. Well, she assumed that, at least. By the time she'd been twenty-one, she'd had a baby and hadn't had much time for dwelling in bars.

"What are you doing tonight?" Cecilia asked as she adjusted Nora's hat tenderly on her head. They were just outside the cafe, preparing to head in separate directions.

"I have my group," Nora said simply, watching as Cecilia's eyes reflected doubt. Nora knew Cecilia didn't think Nora's group was helpful in the slightest; she believed that Nora needed to move on from the past and stop dwelling on the horrible things that had happened. But what did Cecilia know? She'd never lost anything.

"I was going to invite you over for dinner," Cecilia said. "Jax is coming by."

Nora's heart lifted, but she was resolute: she couldn't miss the group. It was her turn to bring a dessert, and she often thought of those people like family — people she couldn't disappoint.

"Give him my best," Nora said. "And tell him to come by whenever he feels like it! I'm always happy to make him his favorite cookies."

"You spoil that boy," Cecilia teased.

That evening, Nora entered the downstairs of the Nantucket Public Library with brownies, lemon bars, and muffins, her eyes alight as she greeted the others walking in alongside her.

"Uh oh! Nora's famous desserts," Addison said as she eyed Nora's platters. "There goes my diet."

"They're literally irresistible," Nate said, coming up behind them.

Nora blushed. "You're too kind."

Together, they ambled into the community room they rented once per week, where twenty to thirty people gathered to discuss grief. Nora began to assemble the platters of desserts on the long table toward the back, listening as people entered the room, greeting one another and asking each other about their weeks and how they'd been.

Nora had joined this grief therapy group twenty-five years ago, during a time when her life had seemed particularly bleak. During the first sessions, she hadn't dared speak about what had happened, nor the fact that she still wasn't sure how to move on. But just sitting in the presence of people who'd also lost someone they'd loved had made her feel less alone. She'd listened to stories from women who'd lost their fiancés, men who'd lost their wives, people who'd lost best friends and lovers, and most excruciatingly, mothers who'd lost their children. Very slowly, she'd begun to understand the weight of her own grief in a way that made more sense to her. She'd been able to carry it a little bit easier. And then, after she'd been going to group therapy for six months or more, she'd finally told everyone what had happened to her, and they'd listened openly and without judgment, which had made her cry until she had nothing left. At that moment, the pressure in her chest had released, and she'd finally been able to breathe.

But that had been so long ago. "Do you still need the group?" is what Cecilia had asked last Christmas, genuinely concerned.

But how could Nora explain that, for her, the grief had never gone away? It had only gotten easier to carry.

Nora found a place to sit next to a woman she was friendly with, who'd lost her husband to liver cancer a few years back. She crossed her ankles beneath her, watching as a woman she'd never seen before entered the room. The woman was young, far too young to be in a place like this, but there was a darkness in her eyes that told Nora she needed help.

"Is this the grief session?" the young woman asked.

"Have a seat," one of the leaders of the group said, gesturing to one of the only open chairs.

The woman hurried to drop herself into the chair and gaze at the floor, clearly embarrassed. Nora's heart went out to her. She remembered how terrible she'd felt when she'd first come, that she'd almost expected someone to tell her to leave because her grief wasn't enough.

The leader that evening started them out gently, then asked someone to share. A man in his mid-forties who'd lost his brother recently raised his hand and spoke very quietly about how much he'd thought about his brother that week and that he'd wanted to call him on the phone several times just to tell him how much he loved him. "We never tell people how much we love them till it's too late," he said simply. "For so many, it's too earnest to scream how we feel to the high heavens. But maybe we should start."

A few other people spoke, discussing what they'd gone through that week, that month, that year, or that decade, sharing bits and pieces of their shattered lives with the group as a way to feel whole again. Nora listened intently. How many people had she seen in this group over the years? Hundreds, if not thousands. It was incredible to imagine how many stories she'd heard— all of which had touched her heart.

A little before they finished for the day, the new young woman raised her hand and said she wanted to speak.

"I'm sorry," the young woman began.

"You don't need to apologize," the group leader said gently. "Why don't you introduce yourself?"

The woman flinched. "My name is Alexa. And I think I must be in the wrong group." Alexa began to stutter. "I um. I've had a hard few months. And they're not sure he's going to make it. But he's still here. My son, I mean."

Nora leaned forward slightly, her mind flashing with images of herself back at the age of thirty-seven— the year she'd lost everything. She'd been older than this young woman, yes. But she'd also lost her son.

The woman's eyes glistened with tears. "He's a toddler. Just the sweetest little boy. But he was diagnosed with cancer a few months ago, and it's been a hard road for both of us. His dad left right after he was born; he couldn't take it. So, it's just been Benny and I, up against the world."

"It sounds like you've been through a lot," the group organizer said softly.

Alexa sniffed. "He's still here. But I hate to say it— I often catch myself losing hope. He's been so sick. And I suppose, in coming here, I wanted to try to prepare myself..." She trailed off, then burrowed her face in her hands.

Nobody knew what to say. It was the first time anyone had come to the group session to talk about someone they were preparing to lose. Still, because many people had lost loved ones to cancer and other illnesses, they understood the density of the grief that came before the loved one passed on. Bit by bit, people began to say what Alexa needed to hear.

"It sounds like you've been so strong for Benny," one woman said. "He is so lucky to have a mother like you."

"These days are not easy," another man said. "And I'm sure you don't feel like you have anyone to talk to or anyone who understands. But you were right to come here. Many of us understand exactly what you're going through."

Alexa dropped her chin and thanked them.

"Don't be afraid to come back," the organizer urged her.

By eight-thirty, the speaking portion of the meeting finished to make time for brownies, lemon bars, and muffins. People gathered around the table to compliment Nora's baking skills and ask her how she'd been, their smiles genuine. Sometimes, Nora wondered if they dismissed her grief since it had been caused by something that had happened so long ago. As she eyed the young woman across the table from her, it occurred to her that she'd lost her son before Alexa had even been born.

"It's good you came here today," Nora said suddenly, surprising herself.

Alexa raised her eyes to meet Nora's. She hadn't taken any dessert. "I feel a bit foolish, to be honest."

"Don't," Nora said. "Nobody else is thinking that."

Alexa tried to smile, but it fell immediately.

"I'm Nora, by the way."

"It's nice to meet you," Alexa said.

"What do you do, Alexa?" Nora asked.

"I'm a painter," Alexa said. "Sort of. I mean, that's

mostly how I made my living before Benny's diagnosis. But since then, we moved back in with my mother and father."

"I'm sure your parents are very happy to have you home."

Alexa nodded.

"I run a small art shop," Nora explained then. "I'm always looking for painters to feature."

"It's an adorable little place," Addison chimed in down the table.

Alexa brightened. "Goodness, that's to kind of you. Let me find my business card." Alexa ruffled through her purse, then removed a card from her wallet, saying, "You can check out my website and see if you actually want to feature my stuff."

Nora took the business card, upon which Alexa had written:

Alexa Jenkins - Painter

alexa.jenkins.com

"Alexa Jenkins," Nora repeated with a smile.

"My mom is actually an art dealer," Alexa went on. "Maybe you know her? Oriana Jenkins?"

Nora shook her head. "I've heard the name, but I don't know her. I mostly deal one-on-one with local artists." She paused, then asked, "Has your mother helped you further your art career?"

Alexa grimaced. "I'm a bit stubborn when it comes to that. I want my art to be successful of its own merit, not because my mother told the right people to like it."

"I can understand that," Nora said. She pocketed the business card, then said, "I'll be in touch about the paintings. I look forward to featuring them in the shop!"

When Nora returned home a bit later that night, she

was surprised to find the kitchen all lit up and the radio on.

"Hello?" she called from the foyer, her heartbeat thumping.

Suddenly, Jax stepped out of the kitchen wearing a big, silly smile. "I'm sorry, Aunt Nora! I used your key under the back mat."

Nora's laughter was light and happy, a rarity in her ears. "Jax! It's you! I thought I was being robbed by a very slow and incompetent robber."

"It's just me, your slow and incompetent great-nephew." Jax stepped back into the kitchen and returned with a bouquet of flowers, which he passed to Nora.

"Oh, Jax! You shouldn't have done that."

"I was sad to miss you at dinner," Jax explained. "It's been a while since we saw each other."

Nora laughed and hugged Jax, closing her eyes as tightly as she could to try to blot out the feeling that Jax was so much like the son she'd lost. "They're beautiful. Do you have room for dessert?"

"Aunt Nora, you know I always have room for dessert," Jax said, following her back into the kitchen. She placed the flowers in a vase and began to pepper Jax with questions about his recent trip to Chicago to meet a friend and, now that it was early July and a fully vibrant summer, what he planned to do with himself. Easily, they fell into conversation, and Nora felt as light as air.

Jax was one of the greatest gifts of her life. She could only thank her lucky stars that he thought of her often and wanted to come by to visit. As far as she could tell, he didn't think of her as a "little old lady"— not fully, anyway.

Chapter Three

Charlie Coleman woke with a gasp. He was covered in sweat to the point that he'd drenched his sheets with it, and his throat was parched. Delirious, he searched through the darkness to find his phone, which showed him it was just past two in the morning.

It took a moment for the nightmares to recede into the back of his mind again. When they did, he shook his head and fell back on the pillow, exhausted. Beside him, his wife, Shawna, turned to look at him, then whispered, "Are you all right?"

Charlie sighed. "I am, now."

Shawna placed her hand on Charlie's chest and rubbed it tenderly, her eyes understanding, but her lips twisted with worry. "Was it the same dream?"

"I think so," Charlie muttered.

Shawna lifted her head to kiss his cheek, then his lips. "I'm so sorry, honey."

"It's okay," Charlie lied because it wasn't okay, and it hadn't been okay for the past thirty years of his life.

Although Charlie had gone on to marry Shawna and have three beautiful children of his own, he was forever plagued with guilt, so much so that he frequently struggled to sleep.

Still, it was a fine price to pay for escaping that night with his life.

Charlie couldn't get back to sleep, so he tip-toed from bed and walked downstairs to sit at the kitchen table with a glass of water and a glass of scotch, watching as morning light slowly churned through the kitchen windows. He and Shawna had purchased this house after the birth of their first baby, Vince, and had gone on to have two other children, both daughters: Sheila and Marcy. It was hard for Charlie to believe that his children were all grown— and in fact, because of his past, he was so grateful they'd made it so far into adulthood, as he knew it wasn't always a given. Vince was twenty-six and married to Lucy; they had twin babies. Sheila was twenty-four and engaged to a man named Jonathon, whom Charlie rather liked, despite having misgivings about his daughters settling down with anyone. To him, nobody was good enough.

And then, there was his darling youngest daughter, Marcy. Marcy was away at Boston University, a junior getting her teaching degree. Marcy was outspoken, bright, and curious— the sort of woman designed to teach kids about the world around them. And since she was a little girl, she'd told her parents she wanted to be a teacher, to the point that they'd gotten her a blackboard and chalk to "play teacher" when she'd turned eight years old.

When six in the morning rolled around, Charlie brewed a pot of coffee and prepared a weary smile for his wife, who would appear in the kitchen soon. When he heard her soft footsteps upstairs, he cracked eggs into a skillet and popped bread into the toaster, pleased that even if his sleeping had failed him, he could take care of Shawna on days like these.

"Wow. Look at this!" Shawna smiled sleepily from the kitchen doorway, then hurried up to kiss Charlie.

"It's nothing special," Charlie said sheepishly as he slid shiny fried eggs onto a plate and handed it off to her just as the toast burst from the toaster.

Shawna placed her plate on the kitchen table, poured herself a mug of coffee, and gave him one of those looks that seemed to go all the way through him. Charlie dropped his gaze, knowing that Shawna understood the depths of his grief, so much so that she knew when to speak about it and when not to. This morning, Charlie preferred not to talk about what weighed heavily on his mind, especially because today was celebratory. After a first round of summer courses in Boston, Marcy was finally coming home.

As Charlie and Shawna ate breakfast together, Charlie wondered how many other breakfasts he and Shawna had had over the years. Thousands, surely. It sometimes boggled his mind that the teenage girl he'd crushed on at the age of fourteen had gone on to give birth to three of his children, had helped him through perhaps a hundred illnesses, and even managed the books for his business— alongside a successful writing business of her own.

It was about her writing that Shawna spoke now as she buttered her toast, her eyes flashing with excitement. Apparently, an essay she'd written about "empty-nester syndrome" had been picked up by *The Atlantic* and would be published in autumn. Charlie smiled at his brilliant wife and said, "I can't wait to read it." To this, Shawna said, "It might break your heart."

All things considered, Charlie and Shawna had taken to being empty nesters easily. They loved one another, had plenty of hobbies, and frequently met with their friends. But then again, there was no ignoring the fact that with their children out of the house, pieces of their hearts had broken off and been scattered. The pain had dulled, but it would never go away.

At nine-thirty that morning, Charlie drove slowly onto the ferry ramp and parked at the bottom of the enormous boat. Shawna adjusted her sunglasses and texted Marcy they were on the road, then smiled brightly at Charlie, looking, at this moment, perhaps twenty years younger than her forty-seven years. Once, Charlie had asked Shawna, "Do I look very old to you?" And Shawna laughed and said, "Getting older together has been the greatest gift of my life."

The drive to Boston University took a little less than an hour. Throughout, Shawna connected her phone to Charlie's Bluetooth and played songs from their past— hip-hop and pop tracks from the eighties and nineties that they sang along to joyfully, remembering how light and free they'd been when they'd first heard them. That was the thing about music— it easily transported you back in time.

Boston University campus was not as vibrant this deep into the summer. A few cars lined the sidewalks, their back trunks open as parents gathered boxes of their children's lives, so grateful to take them back home. Because Marcy was a junior, she lived in an apartment a little outside of campus with two girlfriends, both of whom had decided to stay in Boston for the entire summer. Marcy had considered it at first— which had obviously broken Charlie's heart. When she'd finally said she couldn't imagine missing a summer in Nantucket, Charlie and Shawna had rejoiced. They would have their girl back!

"Marcy!" Shawna cried as they pulled up alongside the apartment building to see their daughter waving from her bedroom window, three stories up. Even from the road, she looked so happy and beautiful, her long hair whipping around her smile.

Upstairs, Charlie and Shawna hugged their daughter exuberantly as Marcy welcomed them with cups of coffee and cookies her roommate had baked a few nights before during a stress bake caused by finals.

"How did finals go?" Charlie asked.

"Not bad," Marcy said with a shrug. "Mostly As. A few Bs. But more than that, my applications for assistant teaching were due this past week, so it was a perfect storm of responsibilities."

"Did you apply around Boston?" Shawna asked.

Marcy's eyes glittered. "Yes. But I made sure to send a few applications to Nantucket and Martha's Vineyard, just to see what would happen."

Charlie's heart lifted. He knew he was lucky to have his two eldest children in Nantucket for the time being. It was almost beyond his wildest dreams that Marcy, too, would take a job there.

Marcy had already packed her belongings in three suitcases and two boxes. Because she'd rented the furniture from the apartment itself, she left it behind, laughing that she wouldn't miss the mattress. "My back cannot wait to sleep in my bed at home."

Charlie, Shawna, and Marcy loaded up the truck,

then Marcy hurried back inside to knock on her room-mates' doors and say goodbye. Charlie and Shawna grinned at one another beneath the beating July sunlight and waited, expectant, until Marcy rushed outside and jumped into the back.

"Let's get out of here," she said. "I'm so ready for summer."

They were off— back the way they came, onto the ferry, then down the ramp and straight for the home Marcy had known since she was a baby. It was three-thirty when they walked through the door, lugged Marcy's belongings to her bedroom, then collapsed on the back porch of the house to take in the afternoon light. Very soon, Shawna rose to pour everyone glasses of iced tea, and Charlie lifted his hand for Marcy to high-five.

"Good work, kid," he said.

"Thanks, Dad." Marcy smiled and returned her eyes to the clouds above. Charlie wondered what was on her mind— if she was still thinking about her semester, if she was dreaming about the summer ahead, or, worst of all, if she was thinking about a boy from Boston University. Charlie wouldn't have dared ask her about her dating life — but he knew it existed. She was twenty-one years old, active, and curious. He wasn't naive.

"We thought we'd head to your grandparents' tonight," Shawna said as she returned with iced tea. "If you're not too tired?"

"No way," Marcy said as she took the iced tea. "I'd love to see everyone. It feels like forever since I've been back." She sipped her iced tea, then said, "Florida for spring break was certainly an experience, but I don't know if I ever need to do that again."

"I imagine the road trip with your girlfriends was a blast," Shawna said.

Marcy nodded. "We took turns driving, and so it made the ride quick."

"You know, you can always take breaks on your way somewhere," Charlie interjected. "I'm happy to pay for a hotel."

Marcy grimaced and sipped her iced tea. "We were fine, Dad. I promise. We would have pulled over if we'd gotten too tired."

Charlie forced himself not to say anything. He didn't want to sour Marcy's first hour home by being a worry wart. For perhaps the millionth time, he considered telling Marcy what had happened in his past, perhaps as a way to remind her to be careful, *really, really careful*, but he figured there was a better time than right now. He always talked himself out of it.

That night, Charlie, Shawna, and Marcy walked over to the house he'd grown up in— the "Coleman House," or so it always would be in his mind. As they walked, Charlie filled Marcy in on more of the details they'd recently learned about his grandfather, Chuck, and the very strange past that Roland and Uncle Grant had hidden from all of them.

Marcy listened quietly as her brow furrowed. "Is Great-Grandpa Chuck going to be there tonight?"

"No. It's just our immediate family tonight," Charlie said.

"And Aunt Samantha was the one who got to the bottom of all of this?" Marcy asked, incredulous.

"She inherited Aunt Jessabelle's house," Shawna explained. "And Jessabelle had left a number of diaries, which explained everything that happened between your great-grandmother and your great-grandfather."

"Another branch of the family," Marcy breathed. "That's so hard to believe, isn't it?"

Charlie grimaced.

"Have you met any of them? I mean, they're Grandpa's half-sisters!"

"My dad seems really hesitant," Charlie admitted.

"He's spent so many years trying to bury the past," Marcy said.

"Especially because he blames my grandfather for killing my grandmother," Charlie continued. "But we also learned that my grandmother had an affair, too, a few years before Chuck's."

"So, you think Chuck had his affair to spite his wife? Show that he could have an affair, too?" Marcy asked, her eyes sorrowful.

"I don't think any of it was kind or good or loving," Charlie said, his eyes toward Shawna, who he'd never, ever considered betraying. "But it's what happened. And now, we're left to pick up the pieces of the past and decide what's next."

"And you want to meet your half-aunts," Marcy said conspiratorially. "I do, too! I'm dying of curiosity."

They'd reached the Coleman House, where they entered to find the entire family out on the back porch, where Samantha's new boyfriend, Derek, stood at the grill, flipping burgers and vegetable kebabs. Recently, their cousin, Sophie, had gone to rehab for a drug problem that none of them had suspected (except Samantha, of course), but she was now back and smiley, speaking to Samantha's daughters on the far end of the porch.

Charlie's mother, Estelle, hurried forward to wrap

Marcy in a hug. "Our girl is back!" she cried. "You've missed quite the beginning of the summer."

"Dad was just updating me," Marcy said, her eyes wide. "How are you doing, Grandma? How's the writing?"

Estelle was an extremely popular harlequin romance novelist, which wasn't exactly a genre Charlie was keen to read, but that didn't make him any less proud.

"Your grandmother got a stack of fan mail this thick this morning," Roland said from behind Estelle, his thumb and first finger wide apart to show off the extent of the mail.

"Do you read all of them?" Marcy asked Estelle.

"I try to," Estelle said.

"She reads them to me sometimes," Roland said as he threw an arm around his wife, clearly proud. "Some of your readers are obsessed with you, honey."

"They are not," Estelle said, her cheeks reddening. "I will say that some of my readers want to control the story-lines, which I find funny. They demand that a character falls in love with another character, stuff like that."

"No way," Marcy said, impressed.

Samantha hurried up after that to hug Marcy, followed by Samantha's daughters, who beamed at Marcy and led her to the corner for summer gossip. Samantha's youngest, Rachelle, had gone to culinary school in Boston until recently, and during their time in the same city, Rachelle and Marcy had run around together. Of this, Samantha and Charlie had winced and said, "I hope they're being safe."

"Hey, big brother," Samantha said with a smile. "I see you brought your girl home."

"We're over the moon. I assume my other children are

on their way?" Charlie scanned the crowd of Colemans, then finally spotted his eldest, Vince, over by the flower bed with two babies in his arms.

"They finally fell asleep," Samantha explained. "Lucy stayed home, bless her heart. She has a cold."

"I imagine she's glad to have a few hours to herself," Shawna said knowingly.

"Having one baby at a time is hard enough," Samantha agreed.

"All right! Who's ready for burgers?" Derek called, his spatula waving.

Everyone hollered that they were ready, that they were starving. Quickly, a sort of assembly line was formed, wherein Estelle, Samantha, Hilary, and Shawna put toppings and condiments on burgers and passed out plates. Throughout the chaos, Charlie's middle daughter, Sheila, came with her fiancé, Jonathon, who shook Charlie's hand as Sheila raced to hug Marcy. Charlie's heart flipped over at the sight of his daughters together again after so many months apart.

Beside him, Samantha and Roland were in conversation, and slowly, their words penetrated Charlie's reverie.

"I don't think we should wait," Samantha said. "Oriana and Meghan have known about you and Uncle Grant forever. And Grandpa Chuck won't be around forever, you know?"

Roland shifted his weight, his eyes twitching nervously. "I know that, honey. I do."

"I saw Oriana at Grandpa Chuck's retirement home," Samantha continued. "She seemed like such a lovely woman."

"I'm sure she is." Roland sighed and palmed his neck, his burger still untouched.

"We'd be there the entire time, Dad," Charlie said. "It wouldn't be awkward in the least."

Roland locked eyes with Charlie, and Charlie again remembered the man he'd once fought with as a teenager — a man who'd had limits to his patience. Now that Charlie was an adult, and his business was even connected to Roland's, they were respectful, never fought, and often grabbed beers together, just as father and son. Still, Charlie lived with a very small amount of fear of his father, something he just couldn't kick from his childhood. He supposed many men were like him: their bodies and their minds aged, but they always thought of their fathers as these big, proud men. It was a funny thing.

"Just let me think about it," Roland said finally, his burger lifted. "I've spent so many years running away from what my father did. I just need a bit of time to process everything. That's all."

Samantha nodded but flashed Charlie a look that told him what was on her mind. That although Samantha and Roland had bonded recently, she still often found him "difficult" and probably always would. Still, because Charlie was a family man to the bone, he was grateful that Samantha and Roland had rekindled their relationship, as living in a shattered family like that had saddened him for years.

Now, they were all together: the Coleman Family, till the end.

Chapter Four

Nora's happy place was her garden. With rows and rows of green and red peppers, radishes, green beans, cucumbers, zucchini, eggplant, onions, and even corn, she was able to eat fresh veggies all summer long and even into fall, at which point she canned and froze a great deal of it to get her through the winter. It reminded her of her mother, God rest her soul, who'd come from a poor family and had learned to make food last.

When Nora had first been married to Jeffrey, they'd planted a garden together their very first spring, working hours in the heat to weed and water the lines of vegetables to perfection. Now that Jeffrey was gone, and Nora was much older than she'd been in the early days of their marriage, it took her more than double the time to care for it.

But on this particular morning in the second week of July, Jax appeared on the other side of the fence in a pair of sunglasses and a tank top and hollered, "Good morning!" in a way that made Nora grin ear-to-ear. She was already out in the yard, a hose raised, which she planned to connect to a sprinkler to give the garden a nice drink. This would help loosen up some of the weeds, which had solidified in the dry ground due to the hot weather.

"What are you doing here?" Nora teased him. "I told you never to come on my property again!"

Jax laughed and stepped through the gate, heading straight for the garden shed, where he fetched the wheel-barrow. "You know how I feel about a full day's work, Aunt Nora. It's good for the soul."

Nora laughed and connected the hose, watching as Jax eased the wheelbarrow to the flower garden along the side of the yard, bent, and began to weed diligently. Nora, who'd spent most of the week alone, now began to plan, with nearly obsessive detail, what she would make for her and Jax for lunch if he decided to stay that long. Oh, she hoped he would stay! She imagined them out on the back porch with turkey and cheese sandwiches and big glasses of lemonade, protected beneath the umbrella over the porch table. She imagined them laughing together, almost as though Jax was her grandson rather than Cecilia's.

Oh, she hated how jealous she was of her sister. She really needed to deal with it, otherwise, it would probably eat her alive.

As luck would have it, Jax did agree to have lunch with her that afternoon. He went inside and scrubbed his hands and his face, then began to slice pieces of cheese at the kitchen counter as Nora washed her hands and tied her hair into a top knot. Jax was telling her a story about a recent beach party, one that all the twenty-somethings on the island attended, and Nora heard herself laughing and asking all the right questions.

"That's when Scarlet Copperfield caught her little

brother with a beer," he explained, his eyes flashing, "and totally freaked out! She put him in the car immediately and drove him back to The Copperfield House."

"Uh oh," Nora said. "How old is he?"

"Sixteen or seventeen, I guess," Jax said. "I mean, Scarlet was a teenager in New York City, so I'm pretty sure she had a beer or two back when she was sixteen."

"She's a protective older sister," Nora said. "I was the same with your grandmother, believe it or not." Nora knew it was difficult for Jax to imagine his grandmother and his great-aunt as anything but old ladies.

"Scarlet came back a little while later," Jax continued as he placed lettuce on a piece of bread, "and she and Marcy became so obsessed with all the constellations in the night sky. Marcy knew so many of them. I couldn't believe it."

Something cold and hard dropped into Nora's stomach. She bit her lower lip, then gazed out the window for a moment, unsure of what to say.

"So, Marcy's back from college, huh?"

Jax eyed Nora nervously, realizing he'd stepped in it. "She just got back."

"And? How is she?" Nora hated the tone she was using, one that made her seem nervous and strange.

"She's good. She's really happy to be back on the island. It sounds like some guy broke her heart back in Boston." Jax said this with relief, as though he was glad someone had broken up with Marcy.

This chilled Nora to the bone, and she frowned, then said, "That girl isn't too reckless or anything, is she?"

Jax's cheeks were pale. "Reckless? Marcy's not reckless."

Nora poured them both glasses of lemonade, her

brain whirring. "I just hope you're careful, both around her and everyone else. I know how those parties can go."

"Aunt Nora," Jax said, stepping up to place his hand on Nora's shoulder. The touch was such a surprise, as she hadn't so much as shaken anyone's hand in about a week. "I'm sorry for bringing up Marcy like that. But, well— what you have to remember is that Marcy isn't her dad. I don't even think she knows about what happened."

Nora turned to lock eyes with Jax. "I hate that she doesn't know."

Jax nodded. "Well, I'm not going to be the one to tell her."

"It should be him," Nora said, her tone very dark.

For a moment, they held the silence. Nora was frightened that Jax would take his sandwich and run out the door, away from this crazy old woman who couldn't escape the pain from her past. But then, Jax did the impossible: he slathered mayonnaise over his bread and said, "What do you want on your sandwich? I'm starving. I might make myself two if that's all right."

Nora sighed with relief. It seemed that Jax would forgive her for anything, including her fears and her sorrows. It seemed that always, he would be by her side, ready to help her water and weed the garden and sit next to her in the sun.

* * *

That afternoon, Jax washed the dishes, hugged Nora goodbye, and then headed off for a shift at a restaurant that had just hired him for the rest of the summer. Nora watched him go from the front window, remembering how she used to watch her own son walk away from the house, just like this, so many years ago. Just before she turned away, the mailman drove up to the mailbox and deposited a number of letters, which Nora decided to grab now.

Nora waved goodbye to the mailman as he drove off, then opened the mailbox to find a number of bills and, incredibly, yet another envelope addressed from Charlie Coleman. Outraged, just as she was every month, she stomped into the house, threw the door closed behind her, and opened the envelope to find a two-thousand-dollar check addressed to her. To date, he'd attempted to send her thousands upon thousands of dollars, but each time, she'd shredded the checks, unwilling to accept his money. She felt that it was dirty. Why couldn't he take a hint?

That afternoon, Nora woke from her nap, showered, and donned a light blue dress, which she wore on her brief walk from the house to her art store. When she arrived, just as they'd planned, Alexa waited with a large box that protected six of her paintings. She smiled as Nora approached and said, "I can't tell you how much this means to me."

Nora slid the key into the lock of the art store, then helped Alexa carry the box of paintings inside. One after another, she pored over the paintings, which illustrated the islands of Nantucket and Martha's Vineyard with inventive colors and unique perspectives.

"You're unlike any of my other artists," Nora said, eyeing the rest of the paintings she was selling in the shop. "Sometimes, I find that lighthouse paintings are a dime a dozen, but yours?" She raised one of them up to really look at it, seeing that Alexa had used purples and greens to create a dynamic shadow, one that made you feel the sorrow and pain of the artist. "Yours are something special, Alexa. I'm so grateful you want to feature them here at my shop."

Alexa and Nora discussed prices for her paintings, all of which Nora felt was appropriate given her audience, and then Alexa admitted that she had to hit the road sooner than later. Her son was back at home, waiting for her. He hadn't been able to keep anything down all week.

"The treatment is so hard on his body," Alexa said, her chin quivering. "It's so hard to see."

Nora nodded and cupped Alexa's elbow. "You'll let me know if I can support you in some way, won't you?"

"You've already been such a help," Alexa assured her.

Nora dropped her shoulders, feeling her story rush to the surface. "I lost my son many years ago. I've learned how to carry it over the years, but that doesn't mean I don't have my bad days."

Alexa's eyes shone with sorrow. "I'm so sorry to hear about your son."

"He was my world," Nora said.

"I know the feeling."

Nora bit her lower lip. "I'll be praying for you and Benny, Alexa. Thank you so much for bringing your paintings today. I'll be in touch when we have our first purchase. I imagine it will be soon."

Alexa thanked her and then fled through the July heat, the box she'd used for the paintings banging against her leg as she went. Nora watched her go for as long as she could until she disappeared around a corner. And then, just as Nora turned away from the window, two customers, an older woman and a younger woman, entered the shop and greeted Nora excitedly. They told her they needed presents for family members who hadn't been able to join them on vacation, and a painting always fit the bill.

"You're in luck, ladies," Nora said. "I've just been in contact with a particularly wonderful artist based in Martha's Vineyard." She then gestured toward Alexa's paintings, which she hadn't had time to hang in the store yet, watching the women's eyes as they engaged with the strange yet invigorating color choices. Within the hour, the older woman had purchased an Alexa original of a field along the southern edge of Nantucket, which dropped into a stony beach, behind which was a violent and black ocean. Unlike other clients, she didn't barter, saying that the piece clearly deserved its full price.

Chapter Five

September 1992

The stands at the Nantucket High School football game were vibrant and alive. Charlie Coleman had just thrown the final touchdown pass to Marcus, and everyone, students and Nantucket locals alike howled from the stands and clapped joyously for their football captain and their whip-fast running back. It was one of those quintessential nights that reminded Nora of being young and free. She missed feeling as though the rest of her life was stretching out before her, as yet untouched by decisions!

Beside her, her husband, Jeffrey, beamed across the crowd. "Can you believe he did it? My boy! My son!" He finally turned to lock eyes with Nora, then he dropped his head and kissed her joyously in a way that reminded Nora of the love that had brought them together and the love they still had.

"He's incredible," Nora agreed with a sigh.

"Hey! Nora! Jeffrey!" A voice rang from a few rows in

the stands ahead of them, and Nora turned to find Estelle Coleman alongside her daughters, Samantha and Hilary. In a flash, Estelle cut through the crowd and took Nora's hand. "Aren't they a perfect team? It's almost like they don't need anyone else out on the field."

Nora laughed, her heart lifting. Ever since Marcus and Charlie had become best friends at the age of five, she and Estelle had been friendly, as well, taking the boys to sports functions and playdates to parks and beaches. Estelle was very intelligent and artistic, which were both things Nora wished she was. She sometimes hoped Estelle would rub off on her.

"Where's Roland?" Nora asked.

Estelle waved her hand. "He's around here somewhere. He wanted to hide from Charlie because he has this theory that if Charlie sees him in the stands, he'll get too nervous and mess up."

"Oh!" Nora laughed.

"There he is!" Estelle pointed at Roland, who went against the stream of high school students and football fans hunting for his wife. "Honey! Up here!"

Roland spotted them and beelined toward them, then shook both Jeffrey's hand and Nora's as he nearly burst with excitement.

"That was quite a pass and quite a catch! I think we should take the boys out to celebrate. What do you think?"

"I'm sure they have their own celebrations," Jeffrey pointed out.

"Always with these beach parties," Estelle said with a knowing smile.

"They won't turn down a dinner with their families," Roland insisted. "After that, they can run all over the island for all I care." He beamed with pride, then hugged Estelle lovingly. "Let's go track them down."

It took a bit of time for Charlie and Marcus to get out of the locker room, and when they did, their hair was wet from the showers, and they wore sloppy, happy grins. "Don't they look the way they did when they were six or seven?" Estelle said to Nora under her breath, and Nora agreed. "Where does the time go?" she asked Estelle, who shrugged.

Nora wrapped her arms around Marcus and gave her congratulations as Roland explained his dinner plans to the boys. Throughout, Charlie gave Roland a confused smile, then said, "I didn't think you'd made it to the game."

To this, Roland waved his hand and explained that he'd watched it from another angle. He didn't mention that he didn't want to make Charlie nervous.

"Is the angle better from there?" Charlie asked.

"It's great," Roland insisted. "How do you feel about a big steak dinner? Huh?"

Within the next half-hour, Nora found herself at a beautiful dinner table at a downtown Nantucket steak restaurant alongside Estelle, Hilary, Samantha, Charlie, Roland, Jeffrey, and Marcus. Lucky for Nora, Marcus had opted for the chair directly across from her, which allowed her to bask in his happiness. Frequently, Marcus and Charlie retold events from the game as though the rest of them hadn't been there to see them, and for some reason, the stories weren't boring at all. Jeffrey and Roland asked all the right questions, both grateful to have such passionate and strong sons.

Nora couldn't help but notice that Samantha, the

middle Coleman, was quiet throughout dinner, moving her food around her plate. Once, when she tried to engage Samantha in conversation about school, Samantha mentioned that she'd decided on a career— that she wanted to be a social worker and specialize in addictions to help people in need. At this, Roland had scoffed and said, "We'll see what happens with that." Nora had burned with curiosity. After all, becoming an addiction counselor seemed like a worthy career choice— one that should have been celebrated. Then again, Roland Coleman was a very proud man who had a vision for everything in life. When he didn't get his way, he pouted about it.

After dinner, Marcus and Charlie announced they had to go. Samantha begged to go along, but Estelle said she was still too young, which made Samantha look dejected.

"You'll have your time," Nora told Samantha, wanting to tell her that life went a lot quicker than you thought— that sometimes, wishing it away was the worst thing you could do.

"Be careful tonight," Roland boomed, locking eyes with Charlie as the teenage boys swept from the restaurant, overwhelmed with passion and energy from their big night and enormous steak meal.

"We always are," Charlie said, flashing that cocky smile of his. Marcus was similar. Nora knew that together, Charlie and Marcus were incredibly popular at school and that many teenage girls had pined for them before they'd both coupled up with their current girlfriends, Shawna and Evie. Nora adored Marcus' girlfriend, Evie, and frequently dreamt that she and Evie were hard at work planning Evie and Marcus' wedding, an event Nora secretly hoped would happen as early as three or four years from now.

"Shall we have another glass of wine?" Estelle smiled at Nora across the table as, directly beside her, Samantha and Hilary locked eyes conspiratorially.

"I wouldn't mind one," Nora told her.

"Mom?" Hilary interjected. "Can we go outside? A few kids from school are hanging out downtown tonight."

Estelle gave Nora a look. "What would you do?"

Nora waved a hand. "I would have let Marcus go, I think."

Estelle wrinkled her nose and leafed through her wallet to give her daughters some cash. When they had it, they raced from the restaurant table and disappeared into the black night, leaving Estelle crumpled and frightened looking.

"I know I shouldn't, but I sometimes want to treat them differently because they're my daughters rather than my son," Estelle explained. "But at the same time, I want them to be confident and self-assured young women. I don't want them to be afraid of the world. It's a tricky line to walk."

Nora could understand where Estelle was coming from. Even though she'd never had daughters, she understood that the world often labeled them "cute," "pretty," or "sweet," and called sons "strong," "fast," and "intelligent." Nora remembered, when she'd been a girl, that her parents had been very cruel to her when puberty had caused her to gain weight that she hadn't been able to lose very quickly. This had set her up for many years of terrible body dysmorphia, which she was grateful not to have passed on to her son. When she'd tried to talk to Jeffrey about this experience, he'd tried and failed to understand. It seemed a uniquely female experience.

Beside Nora and Estelle, Jeffrey and Roland were talking about business. Roland was hard at work on a new construction for a hotel along the coast, and Jeffrey peppered him with questions about construction costs and how many men were required for the build. Roland puffed out his chest, rather arrogantly, Nora thought, and answered every question as though he was the King of France.

"You know, I grew up in Nantucket," Jeffrey began, crossing his arms over his chest. "And I remember that the Coleman name was always thought of synonymously with success."

Roland nodded proudly.

"But back then, I suppose that name was made by your father," Jeffrey continued. "I remember Chuck Coleman well, you know. He always came into the restaurant my father owned when I was a boy and chatted to us about this and that."

Across the table, the light had begun to dim in Roland's eyes. Nora had the strangest sensation that there was something very wrong.

"Anyway," Jeffrey continued, "where is your old man now? I suppose I would have heard if he'd passed on."

Roland coughed into his napkin as, beside him, Estelle stared down at her lap as though she prayed the conversation would end soon.

"My father and I have our differences," Roland said finally.

"As did I with my father," Jeffrey said. "I suppose every son has his problems with his father. Including Marcus and Charlie."

41

Roland's eyes flashed. Nora could see that Jeffrey was making him very angry, and she reached beneath the table and placed her hand on Jeffrey's thigh to try to get him to quit. But Jeffrey pressed on.

"Is he still on the island?" Jeffrey asked. "I feel like I would have seen him over the years if so. But then again, why would a man as beloved as Chuck Coleman leave Nantucket?"

"My family is rather complicated," Roland began.

"As are all families," Jeffrey interjected.

"Suffice it to say that my father no longer upheld the Coleman name," Roland said. "And we decided to cut ties."

"That's rather vague, isn't it?" Jeffrey asked.

Roland sipped his scotch, his eyes scanning the heads of the other people in the restaurant. His smile never fell off his face, as though he was conscious that everyone else at the restaurant was looking at him, the rich and successful Roland Coleman. He needed to be perceived a certain way at all times. For this, Nora pitied him.

"Anyway," Estelle said brightly, leaning forward to take on the conversation. "I don't suppose anyone would be up for dessert?"

A little more than an hour later, Nora and Jeffrey got back in their car and drove to the house they'd raised Marcus in, which was dark and warm beneath the September moon. Nora removed her shoes and walked to the kitchen, listening as Jeffrey removed his autumn jacket and coughed into his handkerchief. How many hundreds of times had they returned home like this? How many more thousand times would they perform these same rituals before they passed on?

"Wasn't Roland so strange when I asked him about

his father?" Jeffrey appeared in the doorway of the kitchen and crossed his arms.

"It was bizarre," Nora agreed. "Can you imagine disowning your father because he doesn't 'uphold your family name'?"

"I don't get it," Jeffrey said. "Then again, Roland is about the most arrogant man I've ever met."

Nora placed a hand on Jeffrey's arm and rubbed it tenderly,

"I mean, what if Charlie wakes up one day and tells Roland he doesn't want him to be his father anymore? Because he's broken some kind of rule?" Jeffrey asked.

"It seems more likely that Samantha will step away from the family," Nora said. "She wants to be an addiction counselor, and her father belittles the occupation."

Jeffrey sighed and dropped into a kitchen chair. Yet again, Nora felt them fall into a similar trap, wherein they discussed how messy the lives of other people were, especially when compared to their own. Their happiness came easily. With only one child, they hadn't allowed themselves to bail on their health or their hobbies, and they'd even upheld date night most weeks the past several years. Their love was strong, alive, and the perfect representation to Marcus of how best to live.

"Shall we have some ice cream?" Nora asked conspiratorially.

Jeffrey smiled. "I thought you'd never ask, my love."

Chapter Six

Present Day

Samantha called on Charlie's way home from work. He had the windows of his truck wide open, and July winds burst across his face, simmering with summertime smells of ice cream, barbecue, salty seas, and fish— so much fish. Charlie answered the phone just as he pulled into his driveway. "Hey, Sam!"

"I'm glad I caught you," Samantha said, sounding breathless. "I'm running around like a chicken with its head cut off today. But listen, Oriana just texted to say this weekend works for them if it works for us. What do you say? Should we go for it?"

Charlie turned off the engine and gazed up at the house he shared with Shawna, his thoughts stirring. "Dad's still not up for it?"

"He said no. Uncle Grant is a maybe, but I think he's leaning toward no, too."

"You would think they'd jump at the chance to get to

know their half-sisters," Charlie said as he stepped from the truck. "Grandpa Chuck's affair was another lifetime."

"People don't really ever get over anything," Samantha said with a sigh.

"Let's have them over. Why the heck not?" Charlie bounded into the house, energized despite his long day.

"I can host," Samantha continued.

"You're the hostess with the most-ess these days," Charlie joked. "That Jessabelle House looks good on you."

"Might as well use this veranda as much as I can," Samantha said. "What do you think? Saturday at noon? That way, if they're feeling strange, they can head back to Martha's Vineyard before nightfall, and we can forget all about it."

"I love the exit strategy," Charlie replied. "I can pick up some fresh fish at the Saturday market."

"You're the best, big bro," Samantha said. "Don't know what I would do without you."

That Saturday, Charlie woke up at six to hit the fresh fish market, where he scoured the stalls for freshly caught sea bass, chatting with the local fishermen who all knew his name. Several chefs from local restaurants were there, as well, eagerly anticipating the high-ticket night ahead, telling Charlie that their reservations were completely full and had been for weeks.

"It's been one of the most successful summers of my career," a chef named Jamie told Charlie, his eyes wide with a mix of panic and excitement. "Every day, I wonder if we can really get through tonight. And every night, I celebrate."

Charlie put the fish on ice and returned home to find

Marcy and Shawna out on the back porch with coffee and yogurt bowls filled with fresh fruit.

"Mom tells me you have a big lunch planned today," Marcy said mischievously. "You nervous?"

"Mostly, I'm curious," Charlie confessed. "I would love to know how different they are from us— or how the same they are. They're family in every way, and yet, they seem to have grown up completely different than Dad and Uncle Grant."

"We were just talking about this," Marcy said, nodding toward her mother. "How maybe, because Great-Grandpa Chuck got to raise children a second time, he tried to do it better, with less pain and more compassion."

Charlie frowned as Marcy continued.

"I mean, I love Grandpa," Marcy said of Roland. "But it's been obvious to me since I was a teenager that there's a darkness in him. Generational trauma is a real thing, you know? I took a class on it at Boston U."

Charlie sat on a cushioned chair beside his daughter, feeling a heaviness in his stomach. Perhaps a stronger man would have now told Marcy the problems he'd had with his father as a younger man, how outraged Roland had often made him. But another part of Charlie felt panicked that Marcy was half-referring to him, to Charlie, when she spoke about generational trauma. He knew it was a fact of life that parents messed their children up— that, alongside their love, they gave them endless neuroses and sorrows and pains. In everything he'd done since Vince had been born, Charlie had tried to be a good father. But he knew that he'd probably come up short.

Around eleven-thirty, Charlie drove up the long and winding driveway to The Jessabelle House, which Samantha had inherited just in the nick of time— immediately after her divorce from her terrible ex-husband, which had necessitated her giving up the house where she'd raised her daughters. During that time, Samantha hadn't wanted much to do with Charlie, nor anyone else in the Coleman Family, and Charlie had felt so helpless as his sister had floundered.

Still, a part of him was jealous that she had such a gorgeous house to herself. The view of the Atlantic was outstanding, and the sunlight hit the veranda perfectly. As Charlie hurried up the steps to the veranda with the cooler of fish in his arms, Samantha came into view at the porch table, which she'd set with real plates and her nicest silverware, her hands blurry as she fidgeted.

"Sam?" Charlie realized she hadn't noticed him, and he didn't want to creep up behind her and scare her.

Sam leaped around, her eyes enormous. "Oh my gosh! I didn't hear you." She laughed at herself and hurried forward to hug him, chatting easily about how much she'd cleaned that morning in preparation for the big lunch. "I don't want them to think we're the sloppy side of the family," she joked.

"I'm sure they're just as nervous as we are," Charlie said.

"Do you think?" Samantha grimaced.

Charlie brought the cooler to the kitchen, where Samantha's daughter, the culinary wizard, Rachelle, was hard at work on appetizers and sides. "Hi, Uncle Charlie," she said, her eyes focused as she gestured toward an empty place on the counter. "Go ahead and put the fish right over there."

Charlie grabbed himself a lemonade and retreated back to the veranda, where his youngest sister, Hilary, appeared in a blue dress and a matching blue hat. Hilary

47

sat on the picnic table and grimaced, her eyes searching the horizon.

"It feels so weird to do this without Dad," she admitted.

"Sophie should be here soon," Samantha said, speaking of Uncle Grant's daughter.

"How are things going with Sophie's divorce?" Hilary asked.

Samantha shrugged. "I don't know. I think Sophie's glad he's not in the picture anymore, though."

"He seemed like a piece of work at your party," Hilary said, referencing the recent Solstice Party Samantha had held at The Jessabelle House, as had been a tradition going back generations.

"That party got summer off to a weird start, didn't it?" Charlie remembered. "Since then, I've felt like something bad is about to happen. There's something in the air."

"Hello?" Sophie called from the veranda steps, where she appeared a moment later, carrying a box of cookies. After her stint in rehab, her eyes were clear, and her smile was sincere and soft. She dropped the cookies on the table and hugged each of her cousins tenderly, thanking them for arranging this lunch with their half-aunts.

"It's so strange. They've just been across the Sound all this time, and we didn't even know it," Sophie finished.

Samantha hurried in and out of the house to fetch appetizers and drinks for lunch as Charlie, Hilary, and Sophie kept their eyes glued to the driveway. Just a minute after the clock struck noon, a car appeared, weaving up the driveway very slowly as though it wasn't entirely sure it wanted to reach the house. It then parked alongside Charlie's truck, then produced two women— both in their late forties or early fifties, wearing straw hats, beautiful dresses, and strappy sandals. Charlie, Sophie, Hilary, and Samantha walked to the end of the veranda and waved down at them, smiling, and they matched them, their faces open and honest and beautiful. It was strange, Charlie thought now, that they represented the reason why Roland hadn't spoken to his father for decades. How could they be the reason for so much pain? They seemed lovely.

"Hi! I'm Oriana!" Oriana Coleman strode up the staircase, adjusting her straw hat on her head and smiling beautifully. She had short blonde hair and a sleek and toned figure, and her smile was a mix of intrigued and sincere. "Samantha, you have a gorgeous house."

Samantha hugged Oriana first, then turned to introduce the others. "This is my big brother, Charlie, my little sister, Hilary, and our cousin, Sophie."

Behind Oriana was Meghan, who seemed quieter and more sensitive, sizing up her newfound family with curious eyes. "I'm Meghan," she said quietly. "It's wonderful to meet you."

For a moment, the six of them were very quiet as, in the distance, the ocean frothed against the stones and rocks of the beach, filling the air with sound.

"My daughter has been hard at work on our lunch," Samantha said finally, guiding them to the table. "She's a student at a culinary school in Boston, which is such a treat for us."

"Does she cook for you often?" Oriana asked.

"She does," Samantha replied. "Lucky me, right?"

"I hope she'll come out and say hello," Meghan said.

"I'm sure she will." Samantha sat at the picnic table, watching the rest of them as they joined her. After a dramatic pause, she said, "I am sorry that my father and uncle couldn't join us today."

Oriana and Meghan exchanged pained glances. It seemed obvious that they wanted to meet their half-brothers more than anything.

"We're just so grateful for your warm welcome," Oriana said, then hesitated before she added, "We've dreamt of meeting Roland and Grant since we were girls."

"When the internet came out, we were obsessed with googling them," Meghan admitted, then giggled.

Charlie frowned. "What stopped you from reaching out to them?"

"Dad explained what he'd done," Oriana admitted. "Which, again, we don't condone."

"The man who cheated on Margaret is not the same man who raised us," Meghan said. "As soon as we were old enough to understand, he expressed his deep regrets for everything he'd done."

"It must have been so difficult to live a double life," Hilary said. "Not only for Grandpa Chuck but also for you both and your mother."

Meghan nodded sadly. "It really hurt Mom when Dad went away. When we were children, we thought it was normal for fathers to leave for many days at a time."

"Why did your mother put up with it?" Samantha asked.

"She loved him so much," Oriana breathed. "And when he spoke about the Coleman Family name..." She trailed off.

"We know all about that," Charlie admitted. "The importance of our family name has been drilled into us since a young age."

"It was poisonous sometimes," Hilary said.

Together, the six of them held the silence, considering the weight of their past. And then, there were footfalls on the veranda, followed by the bright and shiny voice of Rachelle, who said, "I've brought the fish. I hope you're hungry?"

They were all starved. Together, they feasted on the fresh sea bass, potato salad, fresh bread, and roasted peppers as the July sun flitted in and out from behind thick clouds. It was a perfect, seventy-degree afternoon, and, at least for a little while, laughter cocooned their lunch table, saving them from the awkwardness of this meeting.

Still, it seemed clear that both Oriana and Meghan were holding back, as though they weren't sure they could trust the rest of the Coleman family. Charlie thought this was only natural. Perhaps, over time, they could show how open and honest they wanted to be— that extending their family to Martha's Vineyard was a blessing.

"I'm sorry," Oriana stood suddenly, her phone buzzing in her hand. "I have to take this." She then hurried into the house, pressing the phone to her ear.

For a moment, Meghan stared down at her lemonade, her eyes glinting. It was clear that something was wrong.

"I hope Oriana is all right?" Samantha tried.

Meghan shook her head gently. "It's hard to explain."

Hilary and Sophie exchanged glances.

"We know this is a very emotional time," Sophie began.

Meghan raised her eyes to Sophie's. "Yes. Of course." She stuttered, then added, "We have a bigger family dilemma right now. I think we thought, in coming here, we could distract ourselves. But there's no distracting us from something like this."

Samantha frowned and glanced at Charlie, who was at a loss. A moment later, Oriana appeared again, her eyes rimmed red with tears. "I'm sorry about that," she said.

"I hope everything is okay?" Samantha said.

Oriana's cheeks were crimson. When she glanced at Meghan, Meghan nodded firmly as though to say: *just tell them. We can trust them.*

"I don't mean to be dramatic," Oriana began, her voice wavering. "But my grandson has cancer. And it's been a horrific time, to say the least."

"Oh my gosh, Oriana." Samantha stood, her arms hanging loosely at her sides.

Oriana nodded. "My daughter took him to Boston for some tests yesterday, and they're on their way back home now."

"What kind of tests?" Charlie asked, his heart breaking at the thought of a young boy with such a life-altering illness.

"He's been doing chemotherapy for a little while," Oriana explained as she dropped back into her seat. "These tests will tell us if the chemo worked at all or if we need a more advanced treatment." She cupped her hands together and gazed out at the horizon, her jaw slack. "Dad used to talk about this beautiful house, you know. He spoke about Jessabelle all the time, a woman he truly respected, who'd never needed any man."

Samantha flashed Charlie a knowing look, one that reminded Charlie of what Samantha had said about the diaries— that although Jessabelle had built a beautiful life for herself and her career, she'd spent many years very lonely.

"You are welcome here whenever you like," Samantha said quietly. "I would love to meet your daughter, too. And your grandson."

Oriana blinked back tears and then pressed her hands over her eyes. "I'm so sorry to act like this. I thought it would be a good distraction."

"Please, let us know if there's anything we can do," Charlie said.

Meghan reached over to squeeze Oriana's shoulder. They then locked eyes and seemed to have a sisterly conversation in the air, one that nobody else could possibly understand.

"We might head out if that's okay," Meghan said softly. "There's another ferry in a half-hour."

"My daughter and grandson will be home by this evening," Oriana explained.

"Then, you'd better be on your way, too," Hilary said firmly, rising to hug both Oriana and Meghan, who then hugged everyone else, thanking them profusely for the invitation.

"This won't be the last time you're here," Samantha said firmly, waving as they began to walk down the veranda staircase.

"We hope so," Oriana said.

"Text us when you get home safe," Charlie reminded them.

Together, the four Nantucket Colemans watched as the Martha's Vineyard Colemans got into their car and breezed back down the driveway, burning to return to the only home they'd ever known. When their car was out of sight, Samantha heaved a sigh and said, "What a terrible thing."

"I can't imagine what that's like," Hilary said.

Charlie was silent, reeling with surprise and sorrow. How was it possible that the world could be so beautiful and also so cruel at once? How was it possible that you could experience intense and powerful love— and also fall into the depths of sorrow, all within the span of just a few hours? He knew it was the miracle of life, but he also wasn't sure how to be grateful for a beautiful sunrise, especially when it necessitated death and darkness later on.

Chapter Seven

Roland's newest building project was located on an estate that stretched a full two miles along the Nantucket Sound and was therefore owned by one of the richer celebrities who'd decided that Nantucket was paradise. Charlie drove out Monday morning to meet Roland inside the great hall to discuss all things windows and doors, which Charlie provided for all of Roland's builds. His father had gotten what he'd always dreamed of: Charlie was a part of the Coleman Building Empire, if only in a minor way.

Roland was seated at a table, sketching something on a blueprint. Charlie walked quietly so as not to disturb him, remembering the long-lost afternoon when Roland had blamed his son for spilling water on his blueprint. Charlie would never shake the memory of that day from his mind. He still remembered the blueprint, what he and Samantha had spoken about before the game, along with every single play he'd called at the football game itself and everything that happened in the game's aftermath. Carrying those memories around felt like a forever curse.

"Morning," Charlie said when Roland stopped writing.

Roland lifted his head and smiled a smile that showed the depths of his wrinkles, another reminder of how much older he'd gotten in the previous few years. He didn't take as many jobs as he used to, but because he was something of a bulldog, he couldn't "retire" permanently. He just didn't have it in him.

"Morning," Roland said as he stood to shake Charlie's hand. Quickly, the handshake transformed into a hug, which was a rare thing, as Roland so often struggled to show his love, especially to his son. "Check out these blueprints. I think you're going to like the changes I made."

Together, father and son sat together in the as-yet-unfinished "ballroom" for the celebrity mansion, sipped coffee, and pored over the blueprints, which Roland was giddy over. Charlie had never met anyone more obsessed with architecture and design than his father. In fact, he'd taught Charlie everything he'd ever known about windows and doors— which were like added flair to an architectural space.

When Roland finished his presentation of the blueprint, he eyed Charlie and asked, "I don't suppose you'd like to go to Martha's Vineyard with me this afternoon?"

The question came out of the blue. Charlie's eyes widened, and he yearned to ask his father why he hadn't wanted to meet his half-sisters, why he was so afraid.

"Your grandfather wants to have dinner," Roland finished, his hand on the back of his neck. "Grant can't make it, so I thought we could make it a multi-generational affair."

"Sounds good," Charlie said. "Count me in."

That afternoon, Charlie and Roland boarded Roland's sailboat and disembarked, headed westward toward the island that had taken Chuck away from Nantucket forever. When they reached Oak Bluffs, they tied up the boat and hailed a taxi, which took them immediately to Chuck's retirement facility. Chuck was waiting for them in his room, all dressed up in a button-down and a tie.

"You look nice," Charlie as he hugged his grandfather.

"At this age, I don't have a whole lot of reasons to get all gussied up anymore," Chuck explained. "I figured a visit from my son and grandson necessitated a bit of a dress-up."

The taxi remained outside, waiting for them, and after they boarded, it took them to the Sunrise Cove Bistro, where they sat on the back patio with its glorious view of the ocean, ordered water and an appetizer, and looked at one another with a mix of incredulity and gratefulness. Because Charlie had very few memories of his grandfather from his childhood, he felt himself brimming with questions that he'd never been able to ask.

"These beautiful summer days remind me of being a kid again," Chuck said wistfully. "I tell you, I think we were just about as blessed as they come, being born in Nantucket."

"My daughter insisted on coming back for the summer," Charlie said. "She spent the first half of the summer in Boston taking a few classes, but the minute she could get away, she came back to Nantucket."

"Your daughter," Grandpa Chuck repeated. "Tell me about her."

"Marcy is a fiery young woman," Charlie said. "She's

curious and passionate, and she's about one year away from being able to teach professionally."

"A teacher!" Chuck's eyes opened wider. "I just love the sound of her. I hope you'll bring her to visit me one of these days?" He paused, then laughed and said, "Or, heck. I can have one of the girls bring me over to Nantucket sometime. That reminds me. How did Saturday's lunch go?"

Chuck's eyes burned into Charlie's, and Charlie heard himself stutter with nerves. He hadn't brought up the lunch with Roland, careful not to rile him up.

"Oriana and Meghan are wonderful," Charlie said finally. "Although they had to leave early..." He trailed off, remembering the little boy and his cancer.

Chuck's eyes darkened.

"What's going on?" Roland asked, his eyes stirring with curiosity and, if Charlie wasn't mistaken, fear.

Chuck placed his napkin on his lips and drew a breath. "Little Benny was diagnosed with cancer in the spring. He's only three years old, and the news came as such a shock to all of us."

"My gosh." Roland looked flabbergasted.

"Sometimes I feel like the oldest man in the world," Chuck said. "I've hardly ever been sick or injured. It doesn't seem fair that I've been allowed so much health while my young and innocent great-grandson has to live with such tremendous pain."

Roland placed his hand over his heart. In his eyes, Charlie could see regret for having turned down a chance to meet with his half-sisters. Time was all we had, and it often had a mind of its own.

"He's back home now," Chuck said. "We're still waiting on the results of the most recent tests. Gosh, it just eats me up inside." He paused, then added, "I was glad Oriana and Meghan came to see you, though. Oriana's been out of her mind with worry. I think it's good for her to think about something else for a change, even if that something else is what a dummy her father was back in the old days."

"They don't think of you like that," Charlie insisted.

"I know. They've always loved me too much," Chuck admitted. "I've never deserved it."

The waiter returned to take their order, and although Charlie wasn't sure he would ever be hungry again, he ordered a burger. Roland went for the chicken, and Chuck opted for the steak.

"I won't be around much longer," Chuck joked. "And I love a good steak. Might as well enjoy them while I still can."

On the way back to Nantucket, Charlie considered the fact that Chuck was so open with the concept of death. Since everything that had happened back when Charlie was seventeen, Charlie's anxiety around death had been the main reason for the nightmares. He'd even considered going to therapy, but, being a Coleman, he wasn't entirely keen on admitting he had a problem. This pride had been passed down from Roland, who'd gotten his from Chuck.

"How did it feel to see your dad today?" Charlie asked Roland as they eased the sailboat back along the Nantucket docks.

Roland's eyes were misty. "I can't help but think we've lost so much time," he admitted, and then, it seemed as though he didn't want to talk about it anymore. He tied up his rope and stepped from the boat, walking toward his car. Charlie followed behind him, his heart in his throat. He was so grateful that so many years ago when he'd been angry with his father, he hadn't allowed that anger to create a chasm between them. They were still together— they were still here. Charlie had made sure of it.

Because of this, Shawna had suggested recently that Charlie was a much stronger and more open-hearted man than Roland was. Charlie hadn't known what to make of this compliment. On the one hand, he would never believe himself to be stronger or better than his father, and on the other, he prayed that he wouldn't pass down Roland and Chuck's pride to his own children. Life could be tremendously difficult enough without self-inflicted pain.

Charlie said goodbye to his father and drove back home. When he pulled into the driveway, he noticed a car out front he didn't recognize and prepared himself for one of Marcy's girlfriends, maybe Renée, the loud and funny one, or Audrey, the one who looked at Charlie as though she didn't trust him.

But when Charlie entered the kitchen to grab a beer from the fridge, he saw that Marcy and her guest were in the backyard, lounging as the moon rose in the evening sky. His stomach tightened with surprise at the face of the boy with her. It was Jax, whom Marcy had been friendly with all throughout high school. This friendship had, of course, made Charlie incredibly anxious, although he'd tried to shove his fears away at the time. But now that Jax was twenty-one years old, his face had changed and thickened in a way that told Charlie, impossibly, exactly how Marcus' face would have turned out had he been allowed to live longer.

Shame made Charlie's hands drop to his sides. For a

long time, he watched Jax and Marcy in the backyard as Marcy chatted easily, waving her hands in the air to illustrate a story as Jax cackled. It didn't take long for Charlie to realize that they were flirting with one another, that they looked like two people who'd forgotten that the rest of the world existed. Charlie remembered feeling that in the months after he'd first met Shawna. "Man, am I ever going to see you again?" Marcus had joked at the time, jabbing his elbow into Charlie's ribs.

Charlie grabbed his beer and hurried upstairs, holding his breath all the way. When he reached his bedroom, he was surprised to find Shawna there, cuddled up with a book and a glass of chardonnay.

"Hi, there!" Shawna greeted him and slid a bookmark between her pages. A split second later, she frowned, sensing something amiss. "What's going on? How was Martha's Vineyard?"

Charlie sat at the edge of the bed and cracked open his beer, feeling shaken. "Jax is here."

"Yes. I saw that." Shawna's voice hardened. "He seems like a wonderful guy."

Charlie flared his nostrils, not sure what to say.

"I think they might be an item," Shawna said finally.

"I got that hunch, as well."

"Well?" Shawna shrugged. "This isn't such a big island, you know? And isn't it better that Marcy dates an islander rather than someone from Boston? Someone who might take her away?"

Charlie rubbed his cheek, his thoughts ricocheting from ear to ear. "I wonder what Nora thinks."

"I don't know that Jax tells his great aunt everything," Shawna said quietly.

Charlie raised his eyes to Shawna's. "Do you think Jax will tell Marcy?"

Shawna raised her shoulders, and Charlie's stomach felt very cold with the realization that soon, his daughter might look at him as though he was the villain he felt like.

"Maybe you should tell her first," Shawna suggested softly. "There's no reason to run from the past anymore. And Marcy loves you. She'll understand."

To this, Charlie just shook his head, unsure how anyone could possibly "understand" what he'd done. It was a miracle that Shawna had continued to date him after what had happened.

"You should trust Marcy," Shawna said. "Think of all these secrets your father kept from you over the years. You don't want to be like him, do you?"

Chapter Eight

Nora attended her group therapy session that evening, just as she always did, and stood around with a coffee and a cookie, greeting both newcomers and frequent attendees, asking about summer plans and baseball teams and loved ones. Because Nora hadn't baked the cookies, they were dry and slightly burnt, but people forced themselves through them, crunching as they talked. One woman in her forties whispered to Nora, "I wish we could get you to do the dessert every week," and to this, Nora laughed and said, "It's not like I have anything else to do." The woman's eyes were very sad after that, and Nora dropped her gaze, sensing that she'd said something wrong. *Did everyone in group therapy pity her?*

Just that week, Nora had sold three more of Alexa's paintings. One of the buyers, a woman from New York City, had posted about Alexa's painting on social media, and several other buyers had contacted Nora to ask about purchasing more of Alexa's paintings. This pleased Nora to no end, so much so that she'd tried to reach out to Alexa several times to share the news. Unfortunately, Alexa was difficult to get a hold of right now— and this terrified Nora to the bone. Perhaps Benny had taken a turn. Perhaps everything in Alexa's life had fallen apart.

Still, Nora spent the evening staring at the door of the group therapy session, praying that Alexa would make an appearance. When she didn't, she returned home and tried, yet again, to call her, but got no answer. Resolute, she looked up Alexa's home address and decided to close the art shop and go to Martha's Vineyard the following afternoon, if only to give her regards to Alexa and her mother and let Alexa know she cared.

She knew what it was like to lose a son, after all. And she remembered that back then, she'd felt like the loneliest woman in the world.

Nora worked during the morning, then locked the art shop door and walked to the ferry docks to buy a ticket to get to Martha's Vineyard. As the boat disembarked and began to surge westward, Nora remembered the last time she'd been to Martha's Vineyard, long before Jeffrey had ever divorced her. They'd left Marcus with a babysitter, gotten a hotel room in Oak Bluffs, then spent the long weekend traipsing around the island, holding hands, and kissing on beaches. Oh, goodness. She hadn't remembered that in many years, and she hated that the images floated through her mind, now— acting as little knives piercing her heart.

At the Oak Bluffs ferry dock, Nora hailed a taxi and gave the driver the address for Oriana and Alexa's home. As the man drove her, he asked her easy questions about her summer so far and whether or not she'd been to Martha's Vineyard before. Nora told him she was from Nantucket, "the other island," and the taxi driver laughed and told her he'd never been! This was insane to Nora, who heard herself join him in laughter. "Our lives take so many different paths," the driver said as he eased the car into Oriana's driveway. "I hope you enjoy your time on the Vineyard."

Nora shivered before she knocked on the door, unsure of what she planned to say when it opened. A moment later, a woman in her late forties or early fifties answered the door wearing a vibrant smile, peering at Nora curiously.

"Hello?"

Nora stuttered. "Hi! Um. I hope I'm not intruding. I'm sort of a friend of Alexa's. Is she here?"

"Alexa isn't here, I'm afraid," the woman said. "I'm her mother."

"Oh! Oriana?" Nora's voice brightened. "I'm so happy to meet you. My name is Nora, and I've..."

"You're the woman who owns the art shop," Oriana interjected, opening the door wider.

"I hadn't heard from Alexa in a little while," Nora confessed. "I wanted to check in."

"Isn't that sweet of you?" Oriana's eyes widened with surprise. "Please, come in. My neighbor and I just sat down for tea. Would you like some?"

Nora followed Oriana through her ornate foyer, through a beautiful living room lined with incredible paintings and photographs, and into a little nook with a view of the water just behind a line of trees. At the nook table was a man in his sixties with curly gray hair and thick-rimmed glasses. His large hands wrapped around his mug of tea, and he said, "Oriana, I wouldn't have bothered you if I'd known you were expecting company."

"Don't be silly. You never bother me," Oriana said.

"Alan, this is Nora. Nora, this is my next-door neighbor. He just brought me a bunch of vegetables from his garden, and they look divine." Oriana gestured toward the basket on the kitchen counter, which Alan had filled with peppers, onions, cucumbers, and tomatoes.

"They really do," Nora said wistfully. "I've have quite a good spread so far this year, as well. My garden is my very favorite place in the world."

"I wish I had a green thumb like the two of you," Oriana said as she breezed through the kitchen to prepare Nora's tea. "Nora! Please, sit down."

Nora sat nervously next to Alan, crossing her ankles beneath her

"Do you live nearby?" Alan asked her.

"I live in Nantucket, actually," Nora said.

From the kitchen, Oriana explained over the sound of boiling water that Nora was selling Alexa's paintings, which was a great help to Alexa's career during this difficult time.

"She's an incredible artist, isn't she? It was wonderful to watch her grow as an artist from next door," Alan said.

Nora nodded. "I couldn't believe her paintings when I first saw them."

Oriana returned with a mug of hot tea and placed it in front of Nora, beaming. "We're celebrating, Nora."

"What are you celebrating?" Nora asked.

"I suppose you know about our darling Benny," Oriana said. "The doctor called them back yesterday for one final test and then, today, informed Alexa that Benny is in remission. They're on their way back to Martha's Vineyard now. I think Alexa's delirious with happiness."

Nora's jaw dropped. "My goodness! That's fantastic news!"

Oriana clapped her hands as she sat, bubbling with joy. "It's been the most painful time. These past few weeks, we were in a very dark place."

"Gosh," Nora whispered, at a loss for what to say. "Such a little boy should never go through so much."

"I hope that now, he can get back to what he does best," Alan began. "Building Lego sets in the living room that I inevitably step on."

Oriana and Nora laughed gently. Nora then sipped her tea, scalding her tongue, and stood abruptly, feeling as though she couldn't catch her breath. At that moment, Oriana's phone rang, and she said, "That's Alexa. I'll be right back." She then hurried away as Nora focused on filling her lungs.

"Are you all right?" Alan asked kindly.

Nora tried to smile, but she couldn't maintain it. "I'm sorry. I don't know what's happening to me."

Alan stood beside her and touched her back, and the touch sent shivers up and down Nora's spine and along the small of her back. She then locked eyes with him as he instructed her to breathe in and breathe out, on repeat.

"Why don't we go outside?" Alan suggested. "It's a gorgeous day."

Nora nodded and followed Alan through the kitchen and out the back door, where they stood silently and listened to the waves froth along the shore. Inside, Oriana's voice was like a song as she spoke to the daughter who would soon bring her healthy grandson home.

"I'm sorry. I suffer from anxiety," Nora tried to explain because she couldn't say what was actually on her mind. Although she was happy for Oriana, Alexa, and Benny, she couldn't help but wonder why God had decided to spare Benny but take her son. Why had everything happened the way it had? Why hadn't she had one moment of good luck since 1992?

"I think anxiety is an honest reaction to a very difficult world," Alan said.

Again, Nora lifted her eyes to Alan's, surprised at his compassion. "The fresh air helps."

"It's why I spend so much time in my garden," Alan said. "It's the only place I feel like a human."

"I understand that." Nora raised her shoulders, and then, without knowing why, she heard herself say, "Since my son died, I haven't known how to talk to people. I've felt like such a recluse. I have a hard time interacting with others. It's so strange what loss and grief does to a person."

Alan continued to look at her, really look at her, in a way she hadn't been looked at in many years. Although it made her slightly uncomfortable to be seen so clearly, Nora gazed back at him, not wanting the moment to end.

"I lost my wife ten years ago," Alan confessed. "And I haven't felt like myself since."

Suddenly, Oriana opened the back door and said, "Alexa and Benny are on the ferry! They should be home soon. I think we should order food. Lots and lots of food! Alan, would you like to stay? And Nora, you're welcome as well!"

Nora turned to see Oriana, who beamed at them with all the happiness in the world. Quickly, Nora shoved away her jealousy and her self-pity and smiled back, saying, "If I'm not in the way, I'd love to join."

Oriana whirled back into the kitchen and began to make a list of possible menus for the evening— the fish filets from one restaurant, the Indian curry from another, and the Chinese dumplings from another, speaking excitedly and a little too quickly. Nora and Alan returned to fetch the wine from the cellar and help clean the dining room table as Oriana got on the phone with the first restaurant to order enough food to feed a small army. After that, she called another restaurant, where she seemed to know the person who'd answered the phone. To them, she announced the "big news" and then burst into tears.

"Everyone knows everyone on this island," Alan said.

"It's the same on Nantucket," Nora told Alan, although, in her heart, she knew that was true for other people and not her. Perhaps to the rest of Nantucket, she was just that crazy old lady who'd lost everything. Perhaps some children thought she was a witch.

"I'd love to come to see Nantucket sometime," Alan said as he uncorked a bottle of wine and smiled sheepishly. "It's been years since I went out there. My wife preferred elaborate vacations to Europe or Hawaii rather than exploring our own area."

"Europe sounds wonderful!" Nora said.

"It was," Alan said thoughtfully. "And I was happy to make my wife happy, of course. But I always wondered if her desire to travel so far away meant that she wasn't truly happy on Martha's Vineyard."

"It sounds like she was a dreamer," Nora offered.

"Very much so," Alan said, pleased that Nora was willing to speak about his wife.

But Nora understood something many people didn't: that often, the only thing that kept Marcus alive was conversing about him. And more and more, especially this long after his death, people were willing to forget his name.

Chapter Nine

September 1992

Charlie and Marcus waved final goodbyes to their parents as they walked out of the downtown Nantucket steak place, their bellies filled with meat and potatoes and their laughter ringing out through the wild autumn night. Because Marcus' car was busted, Charlie had agreed to drive them all over the place, yet made a point to tease Marcus about it, saying, "I won't take you and Evie out on any dates. You'll have to take care of that yourself." Marcus laughed and buckled his seatbelt, then leaned his head on the seat rest and took in the glowing lights of downtown.

"You got quiet," Charlie joked.

Marcus raised his shoulders. "It was a crazy night, wasn't it?"

"Totally." Charlie started the engine.

"When I reached out and suddenly the ball was in my hands... I couldn't believe it," Marcus said. "I couldn't hear anything. Not the crowd. Not the wind. Just my heart, honestly." He smacked his chest.

"You were faster than I'd ever seen you," Charlie said. "If we'd tried that play even a year ago, it wouldn't have worked half as well."

"Too bad we're seniors," Marcus said. "No more football for us unless we play college ball."

"I'm not going anywhere," Charlie said. "You know my dad would kill me if I left the island."

Marcus remained silent as they drove for a few minutes, snaking further and further out of downtown before they reached the outer banks where all their beach parties were held. Only those in the know at their high school gathered all summer long and even into the frigid autumn to drink beer around bonfires, flirt, kiss, and laugh themselves silly.

Charlie parked the car, and together, the quarterback and his main running back walked toward the party, where, one after another, people turned to greet them and chant their names. "Charlie! Charlie! Marcus! Marcus!" As the sounds of their names got louder, Charlie felt like a king, and he waved, laughing, as Marcus did the same. He knew this kind of "high school power" was finite, that in a year, it wouldn't belong to them anymore, so he was going to enjoy it while he could.

"There he is!" Charlie's beautiful girlfriend, Shawna, rushed through the crowd and leaped into his arms, kissing him in front of everyone. Charlie's heart ballooned with pride, and he whirled her around as everyone watched, probably jealous of all that love and popularity.

Just after Shawna, Marcus' girlfriend, Evie, appeared, and she hugged and kissed Marcus with her eyes closed, clearly swimming in love for him. Marcus kissed her back very quickly, then turned to Charlie and said, "Let's have a beer, huh?"

Evie and Shawna hurried away to fetch them beers, and the crowd parted to allow Charlie and Marcus space by the bonfire. Several people asked them questions about the game, about what they'd been thinking out on the field, and Charlie and Marcus made up elaborate answers, acting like soldiers who'd come home from battle. Charlie watched as Shawna and Evie locked eyes with one another, giggling and rolling their eyes at how ridiculous their boyfriends were. Charlie knew that Shawna would give him heck later for being "so arrogant." But she would do it with love, just as she did everything.

Marcus was drinking quickly. Evie fetched him beer after beer. Charlie stalled after one beer and then finally fetched a second one, not wanting to dig himself too deep since he had to drive. At the beer cooler was a younger cheerleader named Alana Copperfield, who was in a huge fight with her boyfriend, Jeremy Farley, a younger guy on the football team. She pointed her finger against his chest and said, "I think we're through, Jeremy Farley!" And Charlie left as quickly as he could, shaking his head at the drama other couples seemed to have. He was lucky he and Shawna avoided all that. Once, Charlie's mother had suggested he and Shawna were soulmates, and Charlie had wanted to roll his eyes at the idea, but he genuinely believed she was right.

"How was dinner?" Shawna asked when they finally had a moment to themselves, her arms wrapped around his waist.

"Really tasty," Charlie said, then added, "It seems like my dad got out of his weird mood."

Shawna groaned. "You never know which version of

Roland you're going to get."

"I'm seventeen years old, you know? I'm too old to be at the mercy of my father's mood swings."

"We'll get a place to ourselves soon," Shawna breathed tenderly. "And then, you and your father can work on having a healthier relationship. Maybe even a friendship."

Charlie's heart doubled in size at the thought of building a life with Shawna. Obviously, they'd discussed it— especially because the "high school sweetheart" concept was a typical one in Nantucket, one steeped in romance and tradition. Roland and Estelle had been high school sweethearts, as had Shawna's parents. Even Marcus' parents, Nora and Jeffrey, had met as teenagers. Charlie adored the thought that the love you had as a teenager could grow and change along with your relationship— that you could love the same woman throughout so many decades of your life. It was like magic.

Very soon, it was two in the morning, and the winds howled off the Nantucket Sound, threatening to tear through them. Shawna shivered violently in Charlie's arms, and Charlie was overwhelmed with the desire to get her home warm and safe. They had a future in front of them. Besides, Marcus was pretty drunk at this point, and, as far as Charlie was concerned, nothing good could possibly happen after two in the morning. The confident quarterback began to tell others around him that it was about time to "pack it in and go home." Because of his popularity and power, people actually listened and prepared to go home. Only Marcus said they needed more time, throwing his arm around Charlie and saying, "Come on, Charlie, my man! Let's keep this party going all night long."

Evie, who had remained beside Marcus all night, smiled serenely and kissed Marcus on the cheek. "We can all have breakfast tomorrow morning at the diner."

Marcus cast Evie a strange look, one that demanded why she wasn't standing up for what he wanted.

"I think that's a great idea," Shawna said sweetly. "Charlie? Can you drop Evie and I off on the way back?"

"Yeah. No problem," Charlie said, his arm still around Marcus' shoulder as he bee-lined them back toward his car. Shawna and Evie hurried up behind them, giggling together, as, further back, someone else from the high school put out the fire and cast the beach in dark smoke.

"You haven't had too much to drink, right, Charlie?" Shawna asked at the car as Charlie swung Marcus into the passenger seat.

"I had two beers hours ago. I've been drinking water," Charlie said, kissing her gently. "I'm just as sober as I was on the field."

Charlie started the engine and drove them away from the dwindling chaos of the party and out along the dark Nantucket roads back to town, where all four of them lived within a few miles of each other. Throughout, Shawna and Evie teased the boys, and Evie touched Marcus' shoulder frequently, smiling at him through the shadowy car— her reflection often in the rearview mirror.

Evie's house was first. As Charlie stalled the car outside of it, Evie kissed Marcus with her eyes closed and whispered into his ear as Marcus studied the driveway with a pained expression.

"Yeah. Breakfast tomorrow," Marcus said aloud, not bothering with a whisper. "See you then."

Charlie dropped Shawna off next, as she lived only a street away from Evie. Outside her house, he dropped her into a kiss so that she giggled in his arms, then swatted him, saying, "Let me up!" Charlie watched her from the driveway as she slid quietly into her house. A few moments later, her upstairs light went on, and she waved from the window, as was their tradition. He blew her one last kiss, then turned back to get into the driver's seat.

"Jeez, man. That took a while." Marcus gave Charlie a look as Charlie buckled his seatbelt.

"What? Are you in some kind of hurry? I thought you wanted to keep this party going all night long."

Marcus groaned. "I wanted to be on the beach! Not waiting in your car like a sad sack."

Charlie started the engine and began to drive toward Marcus' house, but before he could turn down his street, Marcus waved his hands and said, "Do you mind if we drive around for a little while? I'm not ready to go home just yet."

Charlie eyed Marcus curiously and kept driving, weaving past Marcus' place and back out of town. It was clear Marcus was in some kind of mood, and Charlie wanted to help him out of it if he could.

"Can I ask you something?" Charlie heard himself say.

"Shoot."

"Is there something wrong between you and Evie?"

Marcus groaned into his hand. "I don't know, man. I mean, I love her, I guess."

"You guess?"

"Yeah! Like, I think I love her. But to be honest with you, I've been thinking a lot about my future now that I'm seventeen years old. And I'm wondering if this is all I really want."

"What do you mean?"

"Do I want to stay in Nantucket forever? Do I want to marry the first girl who ever loved me? I don't know," Marcus said.

"Evie's great," Charlie reminded Marcus.

"I know she is." Marcus turned to stare out the window at the fields that flashed past, glittering beneath the moonlight. "I just can't help but think we have this one life to live. I want to get inventive with it. I want to see the world!"

"Don't you think Evie wants to see the world, too?"

"Naw. She wants to get married and have kids immediately," Marcus explained. "Not that that's a bad thing. It will just close other avenues of life right off the bat."

Charlie's stomach tightened at the idea that marrying and having children immediately was some kind of defeated way of living. To him, it was the only way forward— and he couldn't wait, especially with Shawna by his side.

"But think about Nantucket," Charlie began. "It's just about the best place in the world, especially in the summertime. We have everything here. And everyone knows everyone and is always eager to help out, you know?"

"But how do you know it's such a great place? I mean, have you ever been anywhere else?"

Charlie knew Marcus had a point. But more than that, he was bullheaded when it came to Nantucket and his Nantucket family and couldn't imagine seeing the world another way.

"What about your family?" Charlie asked.

"Mom and Dad want the best for me," Marcus said. "And if that means running into the world to see what happens, I think they'd support me."

Charlie wasn't so sure; in his eyes, Nora worshipped Marcus and had done everything to ensure his success, his safety, and his comfort since the day he was born. Marcus had said once that Nora and Jeffrey had tried to have other children, but they'd never come, which had made Marcus their sacred only.

"All right, man. But what about after you run all over the world? Don't you want to come back here? Start a family?" Charlie flashed him a nervous smile, trying to convince him. "I mean, come on. You're my best friend. I need you here. I need our sons to play football together."

Marcus dropped his head against the seat and howled with laughter. "Imagine that. Another generation of Colemans and Fullers out beneath the Friday night lights."

Charlie couldn't tell if Marcus was being sarcastic. It hurt him to think that Marcus wanted to belittle their high school experiences, that he wanted to run off to Paris or Rome or Tokyo to "experience the world" and maybe, eventually, forget all they'd done together in Nantucket.

It was in this moment of naivety, of fear about the future, that everything in Charlie and Marcus' lives changed forever.

Suddenly, out of nowhere, Charlie turned the corner to face a massive pickup truck. The pickup truck didn't have its lights on, and it barrelled directly into the passenger side of Charlie's car, smashing the front and spinning out of control before slamming into a tree and coming to an abrupt stop. Glass shards erupted from the windowpanes, and the airbags exploded into Charlie and Marcus' faces.

A split-second after the impact, everything faded to black, and Charlie and Marcus were just two unconscious boys in a wrecked car on the side of the road.

Chapter Ten

Present Day

It was Saturday morning, and Charlie Coleman stood on his father's sailboat, heading west for Martha's Vineyard. Despite his previous desire to pretend it wasn't happening— that his daughter wasn't fully grown up, it was finally time for Sheila's engagement party to Jonathon, an event Shawna, Sheila, and Marcy had planned obsessively for months. Charlie himself had little idea what they planned for the evening ahead, only that it would be beautiful, elaborate, and very expensive. He was happy to spend every cent in honor of the love Sheila had for Jonathon and vice versa. It just tore him apart to say goodbye to the little girl he'd once known.

A few days before the party, Charlie had called up Grandpa Chuck's retirement home to ask if he wanted to join for the weekend festivities. Grandpa Chuck had leaped at the chance, saying he wouldn't miss it for the world. And again, when Charlie reached the facility to pick him up, Grandpa Chuck was dressed to the nines, looking dapper as ever, his eyes large and excited as they disembarked.

Back on the sailboat, Charlie easily manipulated the ropes and raised the sails, listening as Grandpa Chuck spoke about his great-grandson, Benny, and his cancer remission. "The little boy already has more of a light to his eyes," Chuck explained, his eyes along the horizon as they sailed eastward. "The other day, Alexa brought him over, and we played with his toy trains on the floor for over an hour. Of course, it took me a good thirty minutes to get back up off the floor, but that's life." Chuck cackled, his belly bouncing.

"And what do you think of Sheila's fiancé?" Chuck asked as they eased against the Nantucket docks.

"Good question," Charlie said, flashing his grandfather a funny smile.

"Uh oh," Chuck said. "I know that look. I think I wore it myself when Oriana and Meghan got married."

"It's strange," Charlie confessed. "I'm so grateful Sheila found the one, you know? Because I think, especially in today's times, when people hold off on trying to find their true love for a later date, they never do find the right one."

"I've said it before," Chuck said as Charlie helped him to the dock. "But I'm not sure I believe in soul mates."

Charlie tilted his head. "Why not?"

Chuck sighed and walked along the dock back toward the land of the island he'd abandoned decades before. "When I was married to Margaret, I thought, okay, she's my soul mate. But eventually, we both cheated on each other, right?"

"Right."

"And I found love with someone else," Chuck said.

"But I don't really think she was my soul mate, either. Truthfully, I think building a life with anyone means putting in the work. It means fighting for what you've built together. It means not giving up when times get tough."

"When I first met Shawna as a teenager, I thought for sure she was my soul mate," Charlie said. "And I still think she is, if I'm honest. But you're right. As with any marriage, we've had our ups and downs, and then, sometimes, we've gone even deeper down than that."

Chuck laughed appreciatively.

"But we always came back to each other," Charlie remembered. "We worked on our communication skills. We told one another how we felt and tried to love one another as best as we could. So, you're right. The way I thought about love as a teenager— this 'soul mate' stuff— is overly romantic and not 'real.' True love is work. And I don't think I would have it any other way."

Chuck gave Charlie a small smile, one that warmed Charlie's heart. All his life, he'd wanted to have heart-to-hearts with his grandfather, just like this.

"It sounds like you should include some of that in your speech tonight," Grandpa Chuck said as they got into Charlie's truck.

"You don't think it's too serious?" Charlie asked.

"No. It's beautiful," Chuck said. "And I think your daughter would really appreciate it because it comes from the heart."

As it was still a few hours before the party, Charlie dropped Grandpa Chuck off with his father, where they planned to sit out on the back porch, drink iced tea, chat about Roland's company and Nantucket and Martha's Vineyard gossip, and maybe play cards, if there was time after they got through all the gossip. As Charlie whizzed through the kitchen to get back home to help set up tables and chairs, Estelle waved him down and said, "How's Shawna holding up?"

"She's happy as a clam," Charlie answered. "And nervous as..." He shrugged, unable to come up with something.

Estelle laughed and hurried over to hug Charlie. This close up, Charlie could make out the deep laugh lines on Estelle's face, yet another reminder of all the time that had gone by.

"I'm sure today will be emotional for all of you," Estelle said.

"And it's not even the wedding yet," Charlie joked.

"Just try to enjoy every minute. Sheila and Jonathon will only get married once, you know."

"You don't know that."

"Goodness, Charles Coleman." Estelle rolled her eyes and shooed him out of the kitchen. "Go help your wonderful wife!"

Back at Charlie's place, he found his older daughter and his younger daughter in the kitchen, reading over the seat assignments Sheila had spent "most of last night rear-ranging." He peeked over his daughters' shoulders to see that he was seated at a table with Shawna, Marcy, Estelle, Roland, and Chuck, which pleased him.

"How did it go with Great-Grandpa?" Sheila asked, turning to smile up at her father.

"He's on the island and ready to rock," Charlie joked.

"Daaaaad," Sheila and Marcy sang, embarrassed of him, just as they'd been when they were teenagers.

An hour or so before the guests were set to arrive, Charlie showered in the ensuite bathroom and donned a pair of linen pants and a light button-down, an outfit Shawna had deemed appropriate for the summer engagement party. Just as he finished dressing, Shawna entered the room, already in her light pink dress, looking as beautiful as ever. She paused in the doorway, crossed her arms, and said, "Aren't you a sight for sore eyes?" And then, just as she'd done when they were teenagers, she rushed into his arms and let her lift her in the air, her skirt swirling around her.

"Can you believe it? Another wedding!" Shawna blinked quickly as Charlie set her back down, then said, "I can't even talk about it. I'll start crying!"

Downstairs, Jonathon had arrived with his groomsmen and his parents, and Charlie cleared the back porch to shake their hands. Although Jonathon's grip was strong, his eyes glittered with nerves, and Charlie was immediately taken back to his long-ago wedding day. Although his love for Shawna had been as natural as breathing, it had still terrified him to go up in front of so many people and profess his love for her. *What if he'd tripped? What if he'd said the wrong thing?*

Shawna and Sheila had opted for a wonderful Nantucket catering business, which had already begun to pass out appetizers and cocktails. As guests arrived, they shook Charlie's hand and complimented his backyard, his daughter, his house, his business, and anything else they could think of, their eyes shining. Some of the people who came had been Charlie's friends for decades at this point and had known him through elementary school, middle school, and then, of course, high school.

Although Charlie was used to it after all these years, it always pained him that Marcus couldn't be there. Charlie's life since that fateful night in September 1992 had been irrevocably changed, and he'd carried a Marcus-sized hole in his heart.

Eventually, as he was the father of the bride, Charlie took the microphone to announce it was time for everyone to sit and enjoy the four-course meal. He smiled at the crowd, nearly sixty of their dearest friends and family, and said, "I can't thank you all enough for coming out tonight to celebrate my beautiful daughter and her fiancé, Jonathon."

As everyone settled into their assigned seats, the catering service walked around to fill flutes with champagne, and then, Charlie raised his glass to toast the couple.

"This afternoon, my grandpa and I were sailing back from Martha's Vineyard, where he lives," Charlie began, "and we were talking about the concept of soul mates. It's an unpopular opinion, but we think that soul mates aren't soul mates, per se. They have to be built. They have to be earned. And in this commitment of marriage, you, Sheila, and you, Jonathon, are acknowledging that life is a difficult thing but that you will be stronger and happier if you do it together." He raised his glass higher, his eyes filling with tears. "The greatest gift of my life was watching my children grow up. And now, I get to watch them fall in love and make big, life-altering decisions. What a thing!" His voice wavered and then broke before he hurriedly added, "I'm sorry. I guess, as usual, my wife, Shawna, should have taken over this speech. She's always been better at, well, everything." He laughed, and the rest of the crowd joined in, drinking up the love Charlie had for his wife and his family.

After two of the courses, Charlie excused himself from the table and went inside, where he sat in the shadows of his home, listening to the sounds of the party outside. He could hear Hilary's familiar laugh, then Roland's deep voice, and then, finally, Marcy, giggling over the top of it all.

But for some reason, he couldn't escape the thoughts of Marcus. When he closed his eyes, he could see Marcus in his mind's eye, clear as day, as though he'd just seen him five minutes ago.

Before he fully knew what he'd done, Charlie grabbed his cell phone and dialed the home phone number that had been burned into his mind since the eighties. He knew he would never forget it. As he sat there in the dark, the phone at the house where Marcus had grown up rang and rang and rang, but, perhaps because she had caller ID, or perhaps because she wasn't home, Nora didn't answer it. After the eighth or ninth ring, Charlie hung up and placed his head between his legs, reeling. All he could feel in this horrible moment was guilt. There was no reason that he should have survived that night. There was no reason that it should have been Marcus instead of him.

"Honey?" Shawna's voice rang through the dark hall-ways, and Charlie shoved his phone into his back pocket and hurried to meet her.

"Sorry. I'm back," he said, making his voice bright.

"Oh, good. I didn't want you to miss the next course." Shawna dropped her voice to add, "We picked the roasted ham because we knew you'd like it the most."

"You shouldn't have!" Charlie tried to joke, although his voice sounded strange.

Shawna frowned. "Are you feeling all right?"

"Yeah. I'm just, you know. Nostalgic." Charlie shrugged.

"I know. But you're doing so well. And everyone is having a good time." Shawna rose on her toes to kiss him.

Charlie followed Shawna back into the fray, waving hello to those he passed by and trying to play the "perfect father of the bride." And in fact, he nearly made it the rest of the night just like that, even as they ate cake and ice cream and listened to the music that flowed from the speakers Marcy and Sheila had set up. It was only when Marcy spoke excitedly about her "new boyfriend," Jax coming by for the party that Charlie's heart sank deep into his belly, and he gave her a look that made her own smile fall off her face.

"Are you okay?" Marcy asked.

Charlie palmed the back of his neck. Shawna was right; he should have told his children about what had happened a long time ago. Now, it was an infected wound.

"New boyfriend, huh?" Charlie stuttered.

Marcy nodded excitedly. "I haven't dated an islander since I was in high school. I thought you'd be happy because it means I'll be home a lot more this autumn and winter."

"But Jax?" Charlie found himself searching his mind for a way to push Marcy away from Jax.

"He's wonderful, Dad. You don't really know him." Marcy's eyes had grown suspicious.

"I just don't think you should invite your new boyfriend over tonight," Charlie said. "It's a family party, you know?"

Marcy grimaced. "Sheila really wants him to come."

Charlie nodded and dropped his gaze. He wanted to say something horrible, like, *I paid for this party, so I get to decide who the guests are.* But he wasn't that kind of guy!

He just really didn't want to see Marcus' face floating through his backyard, not now that Marcus was so present in his mind anyway.

"All right," Charlie said with a shrug. "Have a good time."

Charlie kept his distance from Marcy after that. After Jax arrived, Charlie hovered near Roland, Uncle Grant, and Grandpa Chuck, with his back to the party, listening in on their conversations about the old times in Nantucket. At one point, Roland seemed to notice Jax; his face completely changed, as though he'd seen a ghost. But at that moment, he remembered not to bring up any memory of Marcus, as it was too painful for Charlie. Really, it was too painful for all of them.

Chapter Eleven

Nora was in her garden on Sunday morning, her hands covered in soil, her knees planted in the mud. Graciously, a very powerful rain had come late in the night and drenched her vegetables and flowers, and now she tugged at the weeds, listening to the morning come alive around her. Along the fence, a little rabbit bounced and then, upon seeing her, hurried away, frightened, and Nora remained very still, begging the rabbit to return. She wanted her garden to be a place of solitude and happiness for all creatures, not just her.

At nine-thirty that morning, just as he'd said he would, Jax appeared on her front porch wearing that lopsided grin that reminded her so much of Marcus. He hugged her and entered the house like a bolt of lightning, crying out, "I smell bacon! Aunt Nora, I'm starving!" Nora had really missed how hungry young men got. She'd once loved feeding Charlie and Marcus after football practice, as it had seemed, had they not eaten immediately, they would immediately starve.

Jax and Nora sat at the breakfast table together, and

between them, she'd piled platters with bacon, eggs, avocado, various types of cheese, bacon, toast, and vegetables from her garden. It was way too much for two normal adults, but with Jax there, Nora had a hunch they would get through it.

Jax spoke beautifully about his July so far, about the sailing adventure he'd just gone on with a few friends, and about how much he liked his job at the restaurant. Nora told him about Alexa, the young painter, and her son, who'd survived a terrible bout of cancer, and Jax beamed and said, "I'm sure Alexa was so grateful to have your support. It's amazing that you went to Martha's Vineyard to make sure she was all right."

Nora paused, her fork filled with egg, and realized that that day at Oriana and Alexa's had truly been one of the best she'd had in a while. After dinner, Alexa and Oriana had insisted Nora stay the night, and she'd slept comfortably in their guest bedroom, grateful to be surrounded by so much love.

"Their neighbor was very kind," Nora said to Jax now, surprising herself.

"Oh?" Jax gave her a curious smile.

"He's in his late sixties, maybe. A widow."

Jax waved a piece of bacon through the air. "What was his name?"

"Alan." Nora's voice wavered, and she suddenly felt like a teenage girl with a crush.

Jax tilted his head, then took a bite of bacon, chewed, and swallowed. "Can I ask you something? You don't have to answer it if you don't want to."

"Okay." Nora was suddenly terribly nervous. She hadn't had to be honest with anyone in so many years.

"Why haven't you dated at all since your divorce?"

Nora set down her fork and, for a moment, considered telling Jax that he'd crossed a line. But then again, she knew Jax, knew how good his heart was, and that the question had come from a beautiful place of caring for her.

"To be honest, I was scared," Nora answered finally. "Jeffrey really broke my heart when he left, and I wasn't sure how to show myself to anyone after that. For a little while, I wasn't sure if I even was a person after that."

Jax nodded as though he understood, although Nora knew, at his age, it was impossible.

"What about this guy? Alan?" Jax asked. "Would you ever consider going out with him?"

Nora laughed gently. "What on earth would two oldies like us do on a date?"

"Number one, you're not old. And number two, I don't know. I guess you would just do what everyone else does on a date," Jax said. "Go out to eat. See a movie. Go for a walk."

Nora's cheeks burned with embarrassment, but Jax's eyes showed no sign that he was teasing her. He genuinely wanted her to find someone.

"You should be out there dating," Nora said, waving her hand. "Not me."

"I am," Jax said. "Don't worry about me."

Nora laughed, then quickly changed the subject as she slid another egg onto her plate, suddenly ravenous. It had been a long time since she'd eaten so heartily, but it was almost as though that night at Oriana and Alexa's had awoken something in her. When she'd returned to Nantucket the following day, she'd made herself two grilled cheese sandwiches and eaten them back-to-back, smiling to herself. What had gotten into her?

Around one in the afternoon, the surprise of Nora's life came in the form of a text message.

> UNKNOWN NUMBER: Hello, Nora! It's Alan, Oriana's next-door neighbor. I hope you don't mind that I got your number from Alexa.

> UNKNOWN NUMBER: Curious— would you like to go sailing with me sometime? I have an old boat that does the trick. I could pack a bottle of wine and maybe a few snacks. It's not a bad way to spend an afternoon.

> UNKNOWN NUMBER: No pressure, and I hope you're having a beautiful Sunday.

Nora read and reread the text messages, feeling out of her mind. Jax had left only twenty-five minutes ago, after cleaning most of the dishes himself, sudsy water up to his elbows. Now that he was gone, Nora had settled into an armchair to consider what to do next with her day.

But with these text messages, all she could do was obsess about what to do next.

If only Nora had someone to call. Perhaps she could call her sister Cecilia, but so often, she felt Cecilia was too busy for Nora's fears and anxieties, and Nora didn't want to bother her.

Just text him back, Nora, she urged herself. *If you're boring, or if he has a bad time with you, or if he doesn't like you at all, you can just wash your hands of him and never go back to Martha's Vineyard again. Then again, if he doesn't like you, maybe he'll tell Oriana how terrible you are, and then, you'll never be invited back to that warm and cozy home.*

Oh, Nora was going out of her mind with panic.

Quickly, before she could talk herself out of anything, she texted Alan back.

> NORA: Hi Alan! Happy to hear from you. I would like a sail very much. What about Tuesday afternoon?

After Nora sent it, she stared at the text, realizing that Tuesday afternoon was only two days away. What if Alan thought that was too eager? Did normal people have more things to do during the week?

> ALAN: Tuesday is perfect. I can sail to Nantucket and pick you up on the docks. How does that sound?

Nora spent the next two days in a delirious daydream. On the morning of Tuesday, she tried on five different outfits— a blue skirt and a white blouse, a yellow dress, and an orange dress that she immediately threw in the trashcan. Then, she walked to the Nantucket Harbor, hoping the route would calm her nerves.

When Nora reached the docks, Alan was standing on the boardwalk. Although she'd only met him once, she would have recognized him anywhere, with his broad shoulders and his curly gray hair and his thick-rimmed glasses. When he spotted her, he smiled instantly, and Nora felt a skip in her step.

"Hi there," Nora said as she reached him, touching her hair. She'd opted for the blue skirt and a white blouse, thinking it was more appropriate for sailing, and she saw from his expression that she'd chosen well.

"Nora," Alan said her name. "It's so wonderful to see you on your island."

Nora blushed and reached out to shake his hand,

which was a move that immediately thrilled her as though the feeling of his touch ignited something within her. She then followed Alan to his sailboat, where he helped her aboard and instructed her to hold onto the railing. She did, watching as his capable hands untied the ropes and filled the sails and brought the vessel out from the harbor and into the vibrant winds of the Nantucket Sound.

"My gosh," Nora said, her heart lifting. "I feel like a kid again."

Alan laughed. "It always does that to me, too. My father taught me to sail when I was just a boy, and I still remember the first time I ever sailed by myself. I was terrified yet exhilarated, fighting the wind and the water as I went across the Vineyard Sound. When I got back, my father took me out to dinner and told me that I had done something really special one day. Something that I will remember forever. I guess he was right."

Nora beamed at him, trying to peel back the layers of wrinkles to see the face of the boy he'd once been. She supposed he tried to do the same to her.

When they returned to the Nantucket Harbor two hours later, Alan tied up the boat and helped Nora to shore, holding her hand a little too long. Nora beamed at him. She considered telling him that that was the first date she'd been on in decades, but she feared he would say, *I could tell*, which would have mortified her.

"I had so much fun this afternoon," Alan said finally, his eyes widening. "It's fun to sail alone, but it's much better to see everything with someone else there."

Nora's heart opened. "I had fun, too."

Alan shifted his weight. "If I were a younger man, I would ask to kiss you."

Nora's brain was aflame with fear. She swallowed,

searching for the right thing to say, then whispered, "I um." How could she explain how terrified she was? "I need to take things slowly."

Alan nodded. "I suppose I do, too. I'm excited about you, I really am. But I also know better than to leap. You can get hurt if you leap."

For a moment, they held the silence, and Nora allowed herself to hate herself for having said no to a kiss. *Was she crazy?* She'd thought she would never kiss anyone again! And here, this handsome man had actually been up for it!

"Would you like to grab dinner?" Nora asked suddenly.

Alan's eyes softened. "I was afraid the date would end abruptly."

"I don't want that," Nora breathed.

Alan nodded, his shoulders slumping. "Me neither."

Nora turned slightly and tilted her head, guiding Alan down the boardwalk and toward a fantastic fish restaurant, a place she hadn't been to in years because she just didn't have anyone to go with. When they walked in, a waiter hurried toward them and asked if they had a reservation, and when they said no, he led them to two seats at the bar. As they slid onto the stools at the bar, Nora laughed and said, "I feel like a twenty-something sitting at the bar like this."

"Maybe we should sit at the bar more often," Alan suggested. "I don't mind feeling like a twenty-something."

Nora laughed and studied her menu, unsure where to look, as Alan's eyes were too intense for her at the moment. She ordered the cod and asked Alan if he wanted to share some onion rings, her favorite, and Alan jumped at the chance. Nora considered telling Alan that Jeffrey hadn't liked onion rings and that he'd thought they were disgusting. Wherever Jeffrey was, and whoever he'd married after her, she felt bad for him, if only because he couldn't appreciate a good onion ring.

"To us," Alan said as he lifted his beer to clink with Nora's glass of white wine. "And to trying new things. And new islands!"

"Who knew I'd meet someone like you on the other side of the Sound?" Nora agreed, then sipped her wine, her heart brimming over with the impossibility of this happiness. There was no way to know if it would last forever, but at least they could enjoy it in the here and now.

Chapter Twelve

September 1992

It was late, perhaps already one or two in the morning, when Nora and Jeffrey awoke on the couch to realize they'd forgotten to go to bed. Jeffrey rubbed his eyes and winced, saying, "Is Marcus home yet?" And Nora rolled toward him to cuddle close as she whispered, "I don't know. You know how he gets after his football games. It's like he can't calm down."

Nora stood up and walked toward the back window to peer through the black night. Above the island, stars burst in elaborate patterns, and a moon hung too low in the sky as though it planned to drop upon them. She poured herself and Jeffrey two glasses of water, then returned to the living room to see that Jeffrey had fallen back asleep again, his dark hair spilling out across the couch cushion. She felt overwhelmed with love for him.

"Come on, Jeffrey," she breathed, rubbing his shoulder and his lower back. "It's no fun to wake up on the couch in the morning, baby."

Jeffrey groaned and eventually kicked his legs out in front of him, then moved through the shadows toward the staircase. Nora laughed quietly, feeling as though she watched someone sleepwalk, then hurried up behind him, careful to guide him up the steps and toward the bedroom they'd shared for nearly two decades. But just before Jeffrey slipped safely into bed, he smashed his toe on the foot of the bed. His eyes burst open, and he cried out.

Nora dropped onto the bed next to him and hugged him close as Jeffrey began to shake with laughter.

"I must look like a fool to you right now," he said.

Nora thought that maybe she'd never loved him more than right now. "You almost slept-walked the whole way back."

"I just couldn't stick the landing." Jeffrey kissed her cheek sleepily, then asked again, "Is the kid home yet?"

Nora walked to the window to peer down at the driveway, where Marcus' car sat. For a moment, relief came over her until she remembered that Marcus' car wasn't working— that he'd decided to ride around with Charlie Coleman all day and all night. She made a mental note to talk to Estelle about how late they were letting them stay out. Sure, they were seniors, seventeen years old, but that didn't mean they could joyride around the island past two in the morning. They had to be responsible.

Jeffrey fell back asleep easily, but Nora remained awake, peering through the dark and listening intently for Marcus at the door. But two-thirty, then three in the morning, came and went, and her blood pressure was through the roof. She knew Marcus could get carried away, but this was ridiculous.

Nora walked to the kitchen at three-thirty to make

herself a pot of coffee and wait. Down there, she tried to read both a novel and then a magazine about gardening, but the words slipped through her like water through her fingers.

At four-fifteen, the phone rang. Nora couldn't breathe. When she raised the phone to her ear, she tried to come up with a simple explanation for why Marcus was calling so late. Perhaps he and Charlie had done something stupid, maybe snuck off the island for a party or gotten too drunk at someone's place. But the person on the other line wasn't Marcus at all.

"Nora?" The voice was female, and it trembled with sorrow. "Nora, have they come to your house yet?"

Nora frowned, trying to make out who it was. Her first suspicion was that this was a prank phone call. "Who is this?"

"It's Estelle. Roland and I are on our way to the hospital."

Nora's life stood still for a moment, and in that solitary second, she felt everything she'd known about the universe fall apart. "The hospital?"

Suddenly, there was a knock on the door. "Estelle? Can you hold on for a moment? There's someone at the door."

"We'll see you—" Estelle began, but Nora had already put the phone down and begun to float toward the front door. There, she opened it to find two police officers, both men she recognized from around the island, their expressions solemn.

"Mrs. Fuller?"

"Yes."

"Your son has been involved in a major car accident.

He is being treated for his injuries at the Nantucket Hospital."

Nora blinked at them, willing herself out of this reality and into another. "I'm sorry. Can you repeat that?"

Everything happened quickly after that. When the officers instilled Nora with the understanding that this was real and not some nightmare, Nora burst up the steps to wake Jeffrey, who fumbled into his clothing with his eyes half-closed. When they finally reached the car, Nora decided to drive, as she'd already drunk a pot of coffee by then, which gave Jeffrey plenty of time to rant and rave as they hurried for the hospital.

"I don't know why those boys think they can stay out till all hours of the night. Something like this was bound to happen," Jeffrey said. "Just because they rule that school doesn't mean those rules apply to them outside of Nantucket High. Somebody needs to teach them that."

Nora and Jeffrey ran into the emergency room to find Estelle and Roland, both with bloodshot eyes, their arms crossed tightly over their chests as they spoke to a police officer. Nora's legs were jelly beneath her. And then, Estelle turned to look at Nora, to lock eyes with her, and in that impossible moment, Nora knew. She knew in the belly of her soul that Charlie was still alive— and that Marcus hadn't made it.

And at that moment, she hated Estelle for looking at her that way, as though all the pity in the world could bring her son back.

But Jeffrey hadn't caught on to what Nora's intuition had. He stormed Roland, Estelle, and the police officer and began to bark questions. Very soon, a doctor came to lead Jeffrey and Nora away from the waiting room to tell them they'd done all they could in emergency surgery, but that Marcus' wounds were too severe. Jeffrey's first instinct was to insult the doctor, to ask him what medical school he'd gone to. Nora wanted to crawl under the medical gurney and hide from Jeffrey, from the doctor, and from the rest of her life, which awaited her after this horrible meeting.

They were able to see Marcus not long afterward. Nora wasn't sure why they agreed to it; they should have known what they were getting themselves into. The seventeen-year-old boy on the hospital bed, his skin pale and his eyes closed, had very little to do with the confident and powerful young man they'd seen out on the football field only hours before. Nora wanted to tell the doctor he'd made a mistake; this wasn't her son.

When Nora and Jeffrey stumbled back into the waiting room to leave, it was eight-thirty in the morning, and Saturday morning light flooded the hospital. Estelle and Roland were nowhere to be found, and Jeffrey muttered something about Charlie, about how he'd obviously been the one driving. "That idiot killed our son."

Nora's heart felt like it had shattered into a million pieces. A thousand images flashed through her mind of Charlie and Marcus, Marcus, and Charlie: six years old with little backpacks on their backs, waving from the school bus; ten years old, taking guitar lessons that they quit very soon after; fourteen years old and coming into their long legs, their cheeks covered in pimples. They'd always had each other.

According to gossip that swirled on the island, Charlie got out of the hospital two days after the accident. He quit the football team, and his girlfriend brought him homework, nursing him back to health and updating him on what he'd missed in class. Meanwhile, Marcus' room remained just as it had been when he'd left for the football field that Friday afternoon. His jacket was strewn across the bed, a scarf on his nightstand, and a book open on the desk. Nora wasn't sure she would ever be able to clean it up.

Once, Marcus' girlfriend came by and knocked on the door. Little Evie was pale, her cheeks sunken in and her eyes nervous and small. Nora watched her from Marcus' bedroom, willing herself to go answer the door and hug the girl, who so clearly needed support. But Nora didn't have any support to give anyone. She could hardly keep herself alive.

They buried Marcus quietly, as Nora couldn't take a full memorial service, not yet. It was just Jeffrey and Nora at the gravesite, watching as their son was dropped into the earth. Nora's stomach felt cold, hard, and strange, as though her womb was mourning the baby she'd once grown there, and she stopped eating for a little while, to the point that Jeffrey began to scream at her to take care of herself. She did, but only just enough.

Around Christmas that year, Jeffrey ordered Chinese delivery and knocked on the library door to ask Nora to come to eat it with him. On the small television in the library, Nora was watching old Christmas classics that she'd once enjoyed with her mother, and the idea of sitting with Jeffrey and eating anything made her ill. But Jeffrey banged down the door and fell to his knees, begging her to spend a little time with him. It was an act of emotion so profoundly un-Jeffrey that it caught Nora off-guard.

"You've left me alone in this," Jeffrey said. "I don't know where you are anymore."

But Nora had nothing to give him, nor any of her friends, her sister, Cecilia, or her job, or anything for that matter. She felt the days float past and, at some point, knew instinctively that it was time for graduation. That, in another timeline, she would have planned a graduation party for Marcus, had a cake made, and hired a catering service. Marcus had never spoken about what he'd wanted after graduation, but Nora assumed he would have been just like her and Jeffrey— that he would have wanted to settle down and have a family.

Nora couldn't say for certain when Jeffrey first stopped coming home from work on time. She didn't notice it at first, especially because she no longer prepared his dinner and they hardly spoke to one another at all. But night after night, Jeffrey came home at nine, then ten, then twelve, and then, eventually, didn't return till the following evening, caught up in a story that had nothing to do with Nora. When Jeffrey broke the news that he'd been having an affair, Nora said, "Okay," and went up to her little library room and read the journal entry she'd made a few hours after Marcus had been born.

He's our miracle. I can't believe God has blessed me so.

Jeffrey was outside her library door, pounding against it and crying, "Can't we try therapy, Nora? I don't want to leave you."

But Nora had made up her mind that she needed Jeffrey to go. He reminded her too much of Marcus, of the life she'd once loved, and she needed a fresh slate. When she opened the door to peer up at him, she flashed him a sad smile for the first time in nearly a year and said, "Jeffrey, you have to listen to your heart." She'd meant it to sound romantic, but it came out all wrong.

"I am listening to my heart. I want to stay here," Jeffrey pleaded. "This woman— she's in Providence. I met her through work. And, Nora. I don't want to move to Providence! I don't want to move away from you or our son or..."

"Our son isn't here," Nora said, although she knew Jeffrey meant Marcus' grave, which was a place she would never, ever be far from.

Jeffrey dropped to his knees and took her hands in his. "I love you, Nora."

But Nora's heart felt cold and hard, and she couldn't imagine loving anyone, not after her son had been taken away from her. "You should go," she said. "You're still young. You could live a whole new life after this. You could even have a baby."

Chapter Thirteen

Present Day

Wednesday night was date night. Charlie got out of work early, drove home to his wife, then showered and dressed in a pair of linen pants, a button-down, and his baseball hat, which played down the "nicer" clothes and made him feel more like himself. Shawna had already dressed in a light-yellow dress, and her hair was curly and alive across her shoulders. Her eyes danced toward Charlie as she slid earrings into her ears, and she then swung across the room to kiss him with her eyes closed in a way that reminded them of all they'd come from and all they still had to look forward to.

Charlie had made reservations at a little Italian wine bar along the water, a place they could walk to from their home, and together, they linked hands and headed out, through the throng of tourists near the harbor, through the Historic District, past little girls with ice cream cones, tantalizing fish restaurants, the Nantucket Library, the

Nantucket Record's Office, and gorgeous historical buildings that made up the quintessential Nantucket backdrop.

Shawna had finished the majority of her work for their family business early that week to allow her multiple days to focus on a new essay, which she spoke of now with easy eloquence, about the interview she'd had with a poet from Boston and about her search for the perfect words to encapsulate a given emotion. Charlie often had no idea what she was talking about, but he tried his darnedest to keep up. He hoped she knew how much he respected her mind.

At the Italian restaurant, Charlie pulled out her chair and watched as his wife slipped into it, always so graceful. The waiter arrived to take their wine order, and Shawna picked the perfect Italian region. Even the waiter said, "Great choice."

"How do you always know what to order?" Charlie asked.

Shawna swept her hair behind her shoulders, her voice conspiratorial. "You won't tell anyone my secret?"

"No way," Charlie said.

"I researched on something called the 'internet' before we came," she confessed.

Charlie's laughter echoed through the busy restaurant, and several other diners glanced their way, jealous of the happiness that bubbled between them.

"You've got all kinds of tricks up your sleeve."

"I try," Shawna said. "Hey. Do you want to share an appetizer?"

"I thought you'd never ask."

Over a candlelight dinner, Charlie and his forever girl filled themselves with nourishing food, sipped wine, and decompressed after the events of the previous few weeks. They both agreed it had been "one heck of a summer so far" and were amazed it wasn't finished yet.

"Do you think Oriana and Meghan want to try again?" Shawna asked of his half-aunts. "It sounds like the first meeting was really strained."

"I've been considering reaching out," Charlie confessed. "Especially because I think my dad is opening up to the idea more and more. That, and Benny is cancer-free, which is reason to celebrate."

"You know they're always welcome at our place," Shawna said. "I'd love to meet them. Oriana's work in the art world sounds really exciting."

"You're both so smart and artistic. I wouldn't be able to get a word in," Charlie said.

Shawna blushed and sipped her wine. There was a soft, strange pause— one Charlie wasn't accustomed to in their marriage, and Shawna peered into his eyes and said, "Marcy told me she thinks you hate Jax."

Charlie grimaced, remembering the conversation he'd had with Marcy on the night of Sheila's engagement party. "I should have told her about Marcus. I know that." He hung his head, then added, "It feels like it's too late now."

Shawna winced. "I don't think it's ever too late to open up to our children. We're all learning more and more about each other and ourselves as time passes."

Charlie's voice broke. "I'm just so ashamed, Shawna." He was unable to look at her and instead stared through the restaurant, out the window, and toward the violent ocean.

Shawna placed her hand on his. "We haven't really talked about it in years."

"I was hoping I could shove it deep down and never deal with it again," Charlie confessed.

"Right. That always works," Shawna said sarcastically.

Charlie's throat was very tight. Because there were so many other people in the restaurant, he felt safe speaking candidly about his deepest, darkest thoughts. Nobody else could hear him in such a crowded room.

"Back then, after it happened," Charlie began, willing himself to push forward, "did you blame me? I mean, most everyone did."

Shawna frowned. "I didn't blame you, Charlie!" She stuttered, clearly at a loss. "I was with you that night, remember? I watched you drink two beers at the beginning of the night, then switch to the water for the remainder of the evening before we left."

Charlie shrugged. "I wasn't drunk, not even close. But I shouldn't have been driving around so late at night with nowhere to go."

"Teenagers do that all the time," Shawna said. "You and I used to do that constantly, just talking and listening to music."

It was true that Charlie didn't like to do that anymore; that he liked to leave and get to the destination without hesitation.

"And Charlie, don't you remember? They found the other driver at fault," Shawna reminded him. "He spent a few years in prison."

Charlie remembered that, too. He also remembered having learned that the other driver had had to relearn how to walk in prison, which had chilled him to the bone. *Why had Charlie been the only one to recover easily from the crash? Why had he been blessed?*

"Listen," Shawna said, her grip around his hand tightening. "That night in 1992 changed both of us and many other people in ways that we can never take back. Do I wish everything had happened differently? Of course! Did Marcus deserve to die? Absolutely not!" Shawna's eyes filled with tears. "But you don't deserve to put yourself through the wringer every single day just because of another driver's mistake thirty years ago."

Charlie sipped his wine, alternating between feelings of regret and feelings of loss. "I didn't mean to hijack date night."

Shawna shook her head. "You can talk to me about this whenever you want. I'm here for you."

Charlie nodded thoughtfully. "That's the thing. For some reason, I'm the luckiest man in the world. I still have my health. I still have you. I have three beautiful children, a daughter-in-law, two grand babies, and, soon, a new son-in-law, whether I like it or not."

Shawna smiled gently.

"But Nora doesn't have anything," Charlie went on. "She locked herself up in that house and refused to move on from Marcus. She won't cash the checks I send her; she doesn't date. The woman I knew back in the eighties and nineties, Marcus' mother, was always on the move. She was young, must younger than we are now, and vibrant and free. And now? She hates me more than anything or anyone on the planet, and she refuses to move on. And I don't know what to do to make it up to her. I really don't."

Shawna frowned. "I don't know if there's anything you can do to make it up to her. What if something happened to one of our children? Would you be able to forgive someone else?"

Charlie dropped his gaze. "I can't even think about that."

"I know, honey." Shawna exhaled deeply. "But you have to have empathy for Nora. She's doing the best she can. And, for her, 'the best' means staying in that house, selling art in her little art shop, and keeping her distance from the world. Maybe that's okay."

Chapter Fourteen

Nora's Tuesday date with Alan left her delirious with a desire she hadn't previously thought was allowed for someone like her. For hours Wednesday and Thursday mornings, she gazed out the window, watching the sunlight play across the vegetables and flowers in her garden, thinking over and over again about what it might be like to kiss Alan. Perhaps she'd be bad at it, but perhaps that didn't matter. She could tell him she needed to practice, that was all. That it had been a while, but she was willing to work on it.

Why was she so willing to work on it? Nora couldn't remember the last time she'd opened her heart to much of anything. Yes, she'd joined the grief therapy group, which had been a good step forward, and she'd taken a leap to open the art store about fifteen years ago, which had been an act of bravery unforeseen within herself at the time. But a man? A love? Nora hadn't thought herself capable.

For the first time in a very long time, Nora decided to check up on Jeffrey. After his affair, he'd moved to Providence to be with his mistress, whom he'd eventually married. Because she'd been about five years younger than Nora, she'd only been thirty-five when they'd gotten married, and they'd been able to have three children. Three! To be kind, Nora had sent Jeffrey a congratulations card after each of their births, yet had allowed herself brief but exhausting crying sessions, which hadn't really helped.

The man on Jeffrey's social media profile picture was sort of Jeffrey and sort of not. He was older, of course, and a bit rounder; he'd lost most of his hair, and he wore a shirt for a Providence Rotary Club, which wasn't anything Jeffrey would have deigned to join in Nantucket. According to a recent update, one of Jeffrey's children had just had a baby of his own, which had made Jeffrey a first-time grandfather. In a photograph, Jeffrey held the tiniest babe in the world and gazed down at him, mystified.

Here, Nora slammed the computer closed, realizing she'd gone too far.

During those first few years after Jeffrey had left, he'd visited the island to see Marcus' grave often enough that Nora had seen him, sometimes on purpose and sometimes on accident. They'd made it their mission to keep Marcus' grave beautiful and clean and had often grabbed coffee or lunch afterward to catch up. Nora had found it much easier to speak to Jeffrey post-divorce than pre-divorce, as though the act of clearing themselves of each other had cleared the air, too. Frequently, Jeffrey had asked Nora if she was dating again, and Nora had always said no.

Thursday at midday, Alan called her. Nora stared at the phone intently, terrified, then forced herself to answer. "Hello?"

"Nora! Hi!" Alan sounded cheerful. She could

imagine him in the garden in his backyard, a big hat protecting him from the sun. "How are you doing on this fine day?"

Nora smiled ear-to-ear. "I'm just fine, Alan. And you?"

They traded small talk for a few minutes, and Nora's heart opened wider. It seemed easy to banter with him. It seemed easy to tell him how she was and what she was up to.

"Listen. Do you have plans on Saturday?" Alan asked.

Nora closed her eyes. "Not yet," she said, although she never had plans on Saturdays, and this week was no different.

"Oriana is having a party," Alan explained. "Mostly family and friends. After I told her that I'd visited you in Nantucket, she insisted I invite you."

Nora smiled and teased him. "Does that mean Oriana is forcing you to invite me?"

"No! No." Alan laughed. "I would genuinely love it if you came. I could even come to pick you up in the boat if you like."

Nora agreed, then arranged to meet Alan at the Nantucket docks at two-thirty on Saturday. When she got off the phone, she jumped up and down in the kitchen, overwhelmed, then hurried to her closet to figure out what to wear. Because the party was on Martha's Vineyard, she had a hunch she would be spending the night, probably at Oriana's, but that meant there was a possibility she needed a new outfit for Sunday, too. Oh gosh! Her skirts, blouses, dresses, and pants all seemed outdated and worn. Had she actually picked these out for herself?

Nora opened the art shop that afternoon and was

extra chatty with her customers, which she found equated to more sales. At five, she closed and walked down the street to a women's boutique, where she scoured the shelves for a new dress and finally decided on a lilac number with small painted flowers in an ornate pattern. As she gazed at herself in the mirror, the woman who worked at the boutique came up behind her and said, "Most people cannot wear that color, but it's perfect on you." Maybe she was just being nice, but Nora decided to trust her. *Who else did she have to believe?*

On Saturday, Nora donned her lavender dress and a light jacket and walked to the harbor with her eyes peeled for the first sight of Alan's sailboat. When it entered the bay, it moved toward her, bringing the strong figure of Alan closer and closer until she was able to leap onto his sailboat and hug him. He smelled wonderful, like sandal-wood and the sea, and due to her high emotions and the franticness of the ocean, her knees collapsed beneath her. Alan laughed and dropped down to hug her again, then said, "You look so beautiful, Nora." Nora thought maybe he would kiss her then— that maybe she was ready— but instead, he stood and took the boat out of the harbor, heading west for Martha's Vineyard.

When they reached the Oak Bluffs Harbor, Nora and Alan walked to his truck, where he opened the passenger door for her.

"Tell me about your week," he said as he adjusted himself in front of the steering wheel.

Nora's head spun at the idea of telling anyone just how boring she was. "I had a beautiful crop of tomatoes come in this week," she said.

To this, Alan's eyes widened. "I've had terrible toma-toes this year! I don't know what I'm doing wrong!"

Nora beamed, sensing that, no matter what she said, Alan would at least fake an interest in it. "Maybe I can take a look at them this weekend?"

"I would love that," Alan said. "Oriana said you're welcome to stay the night at her place, by the way."

"She texted me this morning," Nora informed.

"I told you. She loves you," Alan said. "She's been nagging me to meet a nice woman for years now."

"Is that so?"

Alan grimaced. "I've known Oriana and her sister, Meghan, for many years. They're a bit younger than me, but they were good friends with my wife." He paused, unsure if that was an okay territory.

"You can talk about her," Nora said. "I understand. She was and is very important to you. It doesn't go away."

At the stoplight, Alan turned to gaze at Nora adoringly. "You don't know what it means to hear you say that."

Alan parked his truck in the driveway of his house, then led Nora inside to fetch a twelve-pack of beer, a dessert he'd attempted to make himself, and a bouquet of flowers. The party, he explained, was a celebration of Benny's health, and he'd wanted his baking skills to show how pleased he was that Benny was now home. "Unfortunately, this might be the saddest cheesecake anyone has ever made," he said.

"The uglier a dessert is, the better it tastes," Nora said. "That's just science."

"Is it? I need to update myself on my science knowledge."

Nora carried the cheesecake and the flowers, while Alan carried the twelve-pack of beer. Together, they moved through the backyard and into Oriana's, which allowed Nora a brilliant view of his vibrant garden. From where she stood, the tomatoes looked excellent, maybe even better than hers.

As they entered Oriana's backyard, Alexa spotted Nora first and hurried toward her to hug her. "I'm so glad you could make it!"

Nora smiled, remembering how sorrowful and gray Alexa had looked not long ago at the grief therapy session. This version of Alexa was completely transformed. "I'm so happy to be here! You must be over the moon right now."

Alexa nodded. "We've taken every chance to celebrate. But now that things have quieted down a bit, Mom wanted to have a full-scale family party to 'officially welcome summer.'" She used air quotes and laughed. "I told her it's already July 22nd, but she said we missed precious summer days due to worry."

Nora knew better than most that worry and grief had a way of robbing time from you.

"Alan!" Alexa moved to hug her neighbor, her eyes flashing knowingly. "Thank you for picking up our darling Nora from Nantucket."

"We can't let her stay over there, can we?" Alan said with a mischievous smile. "I mean, doesn't she know our island is superior in nearly every way?"

"Uh oh. Is this the classic Nantucket and Martha's Vineyard rivalry?" Nora asked.

"You'd better talk to my grandfather about that," Alexa said, gesturing toward a very old man who approached with a cane. "Grandpa? Can I introduce you to my dear friend, Nora? She lives on Nantucket, of all places."

Alexa's grandfather smiled at Nora with a twinkle in his eye. "Nantucket, hmm? Born and raised?"

"Absolutely," Nora said.

"Same," Alexa's grandfather replied.

"But you live on Martha's Vineyard, now?" Nora asked.

"We always ask him which island is better," Alexa explained.

"And I tell you, it's impossible to make up my mind," her grandfather said.

"Do you make it back to Nantucket often?" Nora asked.

"I've been there more often lately," Alexa's grandfather explained thoughtfully. "And it's just as beautiful as it ever was." He paused, then asked, "Could you ever see yourself leaving it?"

Nora bristled, thinking of Marcus' grave, of its constantly required upkeep. "I don't know," she answered for the first time. *Where had that sentiment come from?* She then glanced up into Alan's eyes, which seemed so honest and beautiful, and she felt her soul stir.

Would she ever leave Nantucket for a new life with Alan? Could she even dare to dream of something like that?

"Why don't we get a glass of wine?" Alan suggested.

"That sounds great," Nora said. "It was lovely to meet you."

"Chuck," Alexa's grandfather said, sticking out his hand. "Please to meet you, too, Nora."

At the drinks table, Alan poured Nora a glass of wine and greeted several other party guests by name. Just when Nora assumed he wouldn't introduce her, he did, placing his hand on her back to comfort her. It was as though he sensed how nervous she was.

Oriana soon appeared through the crowd. She wore a white linen pantsuit, and her short blonde hair shone beneath the July sun. In that lush backyard, surrounded by green, she looked like a goddess.

"Nora!" Oriana hurried forward and hugged her. "I was so jealous when Alan said he got a little more time with you."

Nora laughed and glanced Alan's way to see that his face was crimson. "It was a wonderful sailing adventure."

"He knows how to have a good time every once in a while," Oriana teased. "We have your room all ready for you tonight, by the way. Benny was babbling about you earlier, too. 'Where is Nora? Where is Nora?' Apparently, you were quite a big hit the first time you came."

Nora laughed, unsure of what to make of any of this. She felt as though she floated above the ground. Oriana urged them to grab plates and fill up on whatever food they could find, and then, she disappeared through the crowd, eager to make the rounds.

"She seems to have more energy than most people," Nora said.

"You're telling me," Alan said. "It's hard to keep up with her."

"Is Chuck her father?"

"Yes," Alan said. "He's an incredible man, too. I've known him as long as I've known Oriana and her sister. Meghan should be around here somewhere..." He scanned the crowd, wanting to introduce Nora.

But as Nora's eyes followed Chuck's, she peered across the party, which was filled with smiling faces and well-dressed people. It was a Martha's Vineyard summer party at the height of fun, until she found herself locking eyes with someone she would have recognized anywhere.

It was Charlie Coleman.

Nora's lips parted with shock. She blinked several times, watching as Charlie moved along the drinks table with a can of beer in his hand, adjusting his baseball hat. Never did he drop Nora's gaze.

What the heck was he doing there? Rage began to stir in Nora's gut. With her "escape" to Martha's Vineyard, she'd imagined herself running away from every trauma she'd ever known, yet somehow, Charlie Coleman, the reason for all that horror, had wormed his way into her new life. *How had he done it? Was he really that cruel?*

"What's wrong?" Alan whispered sweetly into Nora's ear. "You look like you've seen a ghost."

Nora forced her eyes from Charlie and placed her hand tenderly on Alan's arm. "I'm sorry. I just saw someone I know."

Alan raised his head quickly and searched the party. "Who is it?"

Nora hissed, terrified, "It's Charlie Coleman. But he's a Nantucket resident. What the heck is he doing here?"

Alan's eyes widened. "Oh! He's a Coleman?"

"Yes?"

Alan scratched his beard nervously. "A Nantucket Coleman. Huh. Very interesting."

"Why is that so interesting?" Nora's thoughts raced.

"Oriana and Meghan have always known about their father's 'other family,'" Alan explained. "But that 'other family' only just found out about them. It's been messy, to say the least."

"Wait. Oriana is a Coleman?" Nora's jaw dropped.

"Yes. Her father, Chuck Coleman, moved to Martha's

Vineyard after his first wife passed away," Alan explained. "Once you get him talking about it, it's hard to get him to stop. He's a man filled with regrets." Alan's eyes were far away for a moment, considering the weight of this very old man's life.

But Nora was frozen with disbelief. When she glanced again in Charlie's direction, she found that he'd kept tabs on her throughout his journey across the yard—and that now, if she wasn't mistaken, he was heading right toward her. And she had nowhere else to hide.

Chapter Fifteen

Oriana's invitation made it clear: she wanted to celebrate her grandson's health with both sides of the Coleman family. There was no denying the awkwardness of the situation, but that didn't mean they didn't have enough love to go around. Charlie and Shawna had talked it over for less than five minutes before agreeing it sounded fun. When Samantha and Hilary had texted to say they were in, too, Charlie had arranged for a boat to take them to Martha's Vineyard. Unfortunately, Roland and Uncle Grant had again backed out of the festivities, too nervous to approach Oriana and Meghan.

Now, Charlie, Shawna, Samantha, Derek, Patrick, Sophie, and Hilary were at the backyard extravaganza, which was part celebration for Benny's health and part celebration of all things summer. Yet, unlike his other family members, Charlie was jittery, sweating through all of his clothes. Across the backyard was Nora Fuller, and she wouldn't stop staring at him.

"Hey? You okay?" Shawna appeared beside Charlie and rubbed his back.

Charlie turned away from Nora's penetrating gaze and muttered, "Nora Fuller is here."

Shawna's eyes glowed with shock. "You're kidding! Why would she be here?"

"I don't know," Charlie admitted. "Maybe all this time, she's had a second life on Martha's Vineyard, just like my Grandpa Chuck. Regardless of the why, though, she won't stop staring at me. I feel like she's about to take that cake knife and attack me."

"She's not," Shawna said. "Why don't you just go over and say hello to her?"

Charlie scoffed. "She hasn't spoken to me in more than thirty years."

"Maybe it's time? I mean, she looks like she's here with a date. Maybe things in her life are different now."

Charlie sipped his beer and struggled to stand still. A part of him wanted to turn on his heel and walk as far as he could away from this party, into the ocean if he had to. But another part of him knew that seeing Charlie at this party had blown Nora apart just as much as it had him.

Finally, Charlie set his jaw and walked through the lush grass, pausing for a moment to speak with Oriana, who was effervescent and excited about all things Benny, Alexa, and summer. "I'm so glad so many of you made it," she said. "Although I do wish your father and your uncle could have made the trip."

"They wanted to come," Charlie lied. "But Dad had a million work obligations."

Oriana studied him knowingly as though she considered calling him out on his lie. "I suppose a party like this isn't the perfect time to get together. I hope that, soon, we'll find a way to come together as a family. Especially because our father is getting up there in years, you know."

Charlie nodded and swallowed the lump in his throat, still conscious that Nora's eyes were pegging him. Very soon, Oriana moved on to another guest, complimenting her dress as though it was the best piece of fabric on earth.

"Hi, Nora." Charlie stood about two feet away from her, allowing them a healthy distance.

Nora's eyes glistened with tears, which she blinked away. "Charlie."

Beside Nora, a friendly-looking man with wild hair and thick-rimmed glasses stretched out his hand for Charlie to shake. "My name is Alan," he said. "I live next door to Oriana. I heard you're a Coleman?"

"I am." Charlie put on his friendly voice and shook Alan's hand. "I guess it's no mystery to you that my family just learned about Oriana and Meghan."

"I can't even imagine that," Alan replied.

"I had a lot of questions about my grandfather over the years," Charlie continued, falling into his own past as a way to avoid speaking to Nora. "But my sister, Samantha, recently found some diaries from our Great Aunt Jessabelle, and they filled in some of the gaps."

Alan dropped his chin. "Correct me if I'm wrong, but your father always knew about your grandfather's other family, right?"

"He knew." Charlie's smile fell as he added, "I don't think he knew how to handle what happened."

"How could anyone, when they're so young?" Alan said. He then glanced at Nora, who'd remained very quiet, and said, "And how do you two know each other?"

Charlie's throat was very tight. "Everyone knows everyone on Nantucket."

"Just like the Vineyard," Alan said.

"Alan!" Suddenly, the toddler who'd been very sick, Benny, burst across the grass, his arms flailing through the air. Alan turned and dropped down to wrap his arms around the little boy, closing his eyes.

Charlie's heart swelled at the sight of the little boy, who wore a hat on his bald head. In front of him, Nora's eyes were heavy with tears. Alan then lifted Benny up and spoke to him gently, asking him if he was enjoying the party and what he wanted to eat next. As Benny babbled, Alan walked away, happy to help the little boy get whatever snack his heart desired. This left Nora and Charlie alone.

"He's a really cute kid," Charlie tried.

Nora made a soft sound in her throat.

"It's um. It's nice to see you," Charlie said.

Nora eyed Charlie stiffly.

"How do you know Alan?" Charlie asked, sensing that, soon, Nora would rip into him the way she'd always wanted to.

"He's a friend," Nora said.

"Right." Charlie sighed and took a step back, unsure why he'd thought this was a good idea. He and Nora hadn't spoken for decades— she hadn't cashed a single one of his stupid checks. He knew she hated him more than anyone who had a pulse.

And suddenly, for reasons he wasn't sure of, he heard himself say, "My daughter seems really taken with your great-nephew, Jax."

Nora's eyes became very sharp. "I'm sorry?"

Charlie bristled against her anger. "I mean, it just seems like they're spending a lot of time together."

"Are they?"

Charlie shrugged. "My twenty-one-year-old daughter hardly tells me anything. But I know that Jax comes from a great family, which means he must be a great guy..."

Nora remained very quiet. Charlie felt as though he was drowning. Finally, he raised his hands in the air and said, "Okay. Well, I'll leave you alone." He then turned on his heel and walked away from her, back to the comforts of Shawna.

"That looked rough," Shawna said under her breath.

"It was worse than rough."

Shawna rubbed his shoulder. "It's good that you tried to speak to her. Really. You've done all you can."

Charlie nodded and grabbed another beer from the cooler, hoping his wife was right. Afterward, Samantha and her new boyfriend, Derek, swung by, laughing about a conversation they'd just had with Patrick and Sophie about a movie they'd all seen together. It warmed Charlie's heart to see Samantha so happy with someone, especially a man as kind and loyal as Derek seemed. Patrick, fresh out of rehab, was quieter and softer around the edges than he'd seemed when Charlie had first met him, but he looked at Sophie with all the love in the world. Charlie had learned their affair had gone on for quite a while before Sophie had finally been able to leave her husband, who was verbally abusive.

"Why don't we get some cake?" Shawna suggested, guiding Charlie to the dessert table, where Oriana, Chuck, and Meghan laughed together, a happier version of the family Chuck had left behind.

"What are you three conspiring about?" Shawna teased.

"We're always up to no good," Oriana said, her eyes twinkling. "Charlie, I saw you talking to our new friend, Nora. Do you know her from Nantucket?"

Charlie's tongue tasted like paper. He glanced at Shawna, praying she would come up with something to say, and then, he lifted his eyes to Chuck, who seemed none the wiser about what had happened all those years ago. This wasn't strange. After all, by the time Charlie and Marcus had been in the accident, Chuck had already fled the island to his cozy and beautiful life here. For some reason, at this moment, Charlie felt a bubble of rage build within him. Charlie should have had a grandfather!

Shawna explained that they were friendly with Nora from Nantucket, and then, she guided Charlie away from the desserts and around the side of the house, where she ordered him to drink the rest of her water. "Should we try to get home? I think there's a ferry."

"No. I can handle this," Charlie muttered.

"You look sick, Charlie." Shawna placed her hand on Charlie's forehead and frowned, the way she'd done when their kids were growing up.

"I've just thought about the accident a lot today," Charlie explained. "Almost like I knew Nora would be here. Almost like a premonition."

Shawna's frown deepened. "I really think we should go. Oriana will understand. We hardly even know them yet!"

"Let's stick it out a little bit longer," Charlie said. "All I'll do at home is wander around the house, feeling sad and lost."

Shawna nodded and rose up to kiss him on the cheek,

then the lips. Wordlessly, they returned to the party, then fell back into conversation with Samantha and Hilary, who babbled and gossiped like sisters, a rarity for them. Charlie was accustomed to Samantha and Hilary treating one another like strangers.

"That's exactly what Ava said," Hilary spoke of her only daughter, her eyes wide.

"We should get the girls together more often," Samantha said. "It sounds like they have a lot in common."

"True. But a Darcy, Rachelle, and Ava team terrifies me," Hilary joked. "We won't have any power against them."

Not long after that, Charlie's phone began to vibrate in his pocket. Fidgety, he reached for it and read a number he didn't recognize, then shoved it back in his pocket again. When another call came through a second later, he answered it, ready to tell whoever it was they had the wrong number.

"Charlie? It's Mike."

Charlie froze. It was as though the rest of the world went on without him, talking, laughing, eating, and drinking as he came to terms with the fact that a police officer from Nantucket had dialed his cell number.

"We just went by your house," Mike explained. "When you weren't there, I asked your neighbor for your cell."

"What's going on, Mike?" Charlie's cheeks were flat and cold.

Mike sighed deeply. "It's Marcy, Charlie. She's been in an accident, and she's up at the hospital."

Charlie's head began to pound. Quickly, he dropped

down to place his hand on his knee and stabilize himself. He thought he might throw up.

"You still there?" Mike asked.

"I'm here," Charlie rasped.

Shawna was beside him now, her hand on his upper back as she said something to him, something Charlie couldn't understand.

"Is she all right, Mike? Tell it to me straight."

Shawna looked stricken. She placed her hand on her mouth and wavered in place.

"It was a bad one, Charlie," Mike said. "She's still in surgery. The doctor will tell you more when you get there."

Charlie hung up the call and dropped his phone on the grass. Shawna gripped his hand, then wrapped her arms around his waist, shivering as she asked him what had happened. Charlie heard himself mutter the basics— Marcy, car accident— as he hunted for his belongings and explained to Samantha and Hilary that he needed to get back to Nantucket immediately. Samantha and Hilary burst into action to collect Sophie, Patrick, and Derek.

But in the chaos, Charlie raised his eyes across the party and locked them with Nora's, who was white as a sheet. Beside her, Alan looked frightened as well, as he whispered into her ear as they walked toward the backyard next door.

And at that moment, Charlie realized the impossible — that Marcy hadn't been alone in the car accident. That she'd probably been with her boyfriend, Jax. And that history had repeated itself in all its monstrous proportions.

Chapter Sixteen

lthough Charlie had been the one to rent the
boat, he was too out of his mind to chart the
course back to Nantucket. Derek took the
wheel, his eyes nervous as he pulsed them through the
water. The sky had changed, becoming clotted with
bulbous clouds that surged with pink and blue light from
the approaching sunset, and the sea shifted menacingly
beneath them, reminding Charlie that people only ever
pretended to have control over their lives. In reality, life
had its way with you— it took the people you loved the
most, and it robbed you of happiness as a kind of sport.

Throughout the route, Charlie sat next to Shawna,
who looked resolute, her eyes on the horizon. Shawna
wasn't the kind of woman who wanted to talk about her
deepest fears, although she had them. She believed in the
power of the mind and spirit, and she often wrote an affir-
mation and an intention in a journal every morning as a
way to direct her energy toward a single mission. Still,
Shawna's hand around Charlie's was powerful, as though
she clung to him as a way to keep herself sane.

The others on the boat were quiet, understanding that this wasn't the kind of thing you could talk yourself out of.

When Derek slid the boat back into its dock, the man they'd rented it from approached with a smile and said, "You are back early!" Derek said something to him, something that assured everything had gone all right, as Charlie and Shawna hurried onto the docks.

"We'll meet you at the hospital!" Samantha called as they ran.

Charlie turned back and nodded once, then continued on. He wasn't sure he remembered how to drive.

And in fact, the drive to the hospital felt like a dream. Now that they were alone for the first time since they'd learned the news, Shawna burst into spontaneous tears, then tidied herself up.

"We don't know how bad it is yet," she said softly. "We have to stay strong for Marcy."

Charlie nodded, then said, "I think she might have been with Jax."

"I'm sure she was."

Charlie smashed his palm against the steering wheel, overwhelmed with rage and fear. "Do you think he was driving?"

Shawna raised her shoulders. "It doesn't matter, Charlie."

Charlie took a deep breath, but it did little to calm him. In truth, deep within his conscious mind, he erupted with anger toward Jax. Charlie's imagination had gotten the better of him, and he pictured Jax running a red light or speeding to one hundred and fifteen m.p.h. and laughing about it or leaning over to kiss Marcy when he should have been paying attention to the road. *What kind of driving school had given that clown a driver's license? Wasn't it clear he wasn't responsible enough?*

Charlie parked at the hospital, and together, he and Shawna hurried into the waiting room and up to the counter. Throughout, Charlie was filled with images of that long-ago night when he'd been able to walk from that very waiting room back to his parents' car, as his best friend's body had remained behind.

The nurse at the front desk explained that Marcy was still in surgery and that the doctor would come to speak to them immediately afterward. Charlie pressed the nurse for more information, but she didn't have much— just that the accident had occurred on a back country road and that the young man who'd been driving hadn't sustained any life-threatening injuries. She nodded toward the waiting area, where Charlie now saw Jax sitting with his head between his legs. From here, he could see that Jax had a cut on his forehead, and the blood had matted his hair.

Shawna gripped Charlie's arm, trying to hold him back, but it was no use. Charlie stomped toward the young man, the young man who looked just like Marcus, and stopped about five feet in front of him, heaving with anger.

"Jax?" Charlie didn't recognize his own voice.

Slowly, Jax raised his chin to show the beginnings of a black eye and another few cuts around his lips and his neck. His t-shirt was covered in blood, as well.

"Jax, what the heck happened?" Charlie demanded.

Jax opened his lips to speak, but they quivered uncontrollably.

"Answer me!" Charlie demanded of him, then

closed his mouth and turned around, pressing his hands against his face. He couldn't shake the feeling that now, instead of Jax, he was screaming at Marcus. It was as though he'd been pulled through time, all the way back to 1992.

Suddenly, Shawna was before him, and she gathered him in her arms, guiding him to a private corner in the emergency room, where they held each other in the shadows and listened to the sounds of medical machines beeping in the distance and babies crying and sick people wailing. For a long time, neither of them spoke as Charlie stirred with the realization that this was payment for what he'd done all those years ago. That although he'd never meant to get into that accident with Marcus, it was still partially his fault, anyway. Maybe he'd been driving too quickly. Maybe he hadn't been careful enough. And because of his actions, Nora lost her son and her husband, and Marcus lost his life.

Shawna led Charlie to the single-person bathroom, where she collected water in her hands and spread it along his neck and beneath his t-shirt. Charlie moaned and closed his eyes. The nerves had made him sweat through his t-shirt. Quickly, he dunked his face under the faucet and opened his eyes, wishing he could clean his brain of so many painful memories.

Shawna held Charlie's hands and gazed into his eyes. It was clear she was hanging by a thread, just as he was. "Let's leave Jax alone for now, okay?"

Charlie nodded. "I almost lost my head."

"It's understandable," Shawna whispered. "But he looks rough. I don't think he can handle any questions right now."

Charlie wanted to say, *tough luck. We deserve*

answers. But he held it in, knowing his rage would only upset Shawna more.

When Charlie and Shawna left the bathroom, Samantha, Hilary, Roland, Estelle, Vince, and Sheila were gathered outside. The sight of his two other children nearly brought Charlie to his knees. In the darkness of the back of the parking lot, Charlie explained what he knew so far, which was not much. He restrained himself from telling them Jax had been driving. He knew it didn't matter.

Sheila was despondent, weeping against Shawna's shoulder about her sister. Roland and Estelle looked traumatized, probably remembering the night thirty years ago better than Charlie currently did. Roland wrapped his arms around Estelle and held her. Nobody knew quite what to say.

Marcy got out of surgery at midnight, at which time the doctor told Charlie that Marcy was in a coma and very well could be for a number of days, even weeks.

"But she'll come out of the coma?" Charlie demanded.

"We never know what will come of these situations," the doctor explained. "Her body responded well to surgery, but now it's up to her body to heal enough for her to wake up again."

Charlie pressed his hands over his eyes until he saw black spots. Beside him, Shawna asked the doctor if they could sit with Marcy for a little while, and the doctor said of course. Like two zombies, Charlie and Shawna walked down the hallway, then entered their daughter's hospital room and sat by her side, gazing at the beautiful young woman they'd once created, covered in bandages from her face to her wrist to her legs. Machines beside her beeped and pumped, and a chart on the bedside table told of medicines and treatments she'd already received. Charlie bent to kiss her hand, praying that somewhere in there, she felt how much he loved her. Maybe that love would be enough for her to return to him.

Chapter Seventeen

It had been three days since Jax and Marcy's accident, and since then, Nora had heard very little from Jax and had gleaned as much information about Marcy's wellness from Cecilia as she could. At Cecilia's house, she slid a slice of lemon cake onto Nora's plate and placed it in front of her, and Nora forced herself to ask Cecilia an appropriate number of normal questions before she jumped to Jax and Marcy, the real reason for her visit.

Cecilia could talk about anything. She could speak about a butterfly she'd seen in her garden five years ago for at least a half hour, then discuss the rock it had sat on for another twenty minutes. Nora, who wasn't much of a talker at all, tried to listen to Cecilia, reminding herself that Cecilia was one of the only family members she had left.

"Are you all right, Nora? You look a little lost." Cecilia sipped her coffee and gave Nora a nervous smile.

"Lost? No." Nora smiled back.

"You know, a neighbor of mine told me she saw you out in a restaurant with a man," Cecilia said.

Nora's cheeks were aflame with embarrassment. *How was it that the island saw everything she was up to?*

"Who is this handsome gentleman?" Cecilia asked. "My neighbor made sure to say he was incredibly good-looking."

Nora slid her fork through the lemon cake and considered how to tell her sister about the single greatest person to enter her life in decades. *How could she taint the subject of Alan with silly afternoon gossip?* Then again, after Nora had fled Alan's home like a wild woman Saturday night due to fear surrounding Jax's accident, she wasn't sure Alan would ever want to call her again. He certainly hadn't yet.

"He's just a friend," Nora began. "I met him through a young painter who lives on Martha's Vineyard. I sold several of her paintings at the art shop."

Cecilia's eyes widened. "He's a Vineyard resident?"

"Absolutely." Nora straightened her back, then added, "He lost his wife ten years ago."

"Terrible," Cecilia said, although she didn't sound as though she cared. She had never lost anyone dear to her. She had no idea what it was like. "Has it been difficult for you to date again? I imagine you haven't been out on a date in what? Thirty years? More?"

Nora bristled and placed her fork back down, no longer hungry for cake. It felt like her sister was poking at her emotional injuries until they bruised even more.

"Just curious, of course," Cecilia continued. "I don't mean to be rude. I just can't imagine dating at our age."

Nora blinked several times, then heard herself ask,

"Do you know anything more about Jax? Is he holding up okay?"

"Jax?" Cecilia frowned. "Well, my daughter tells me he hasn't spent much time outside of that hospital. I don't think it's very healthy for him to stay inside all the time, especially when the doctors don't know whether or not the girl will wake up."

Nora's stomach tied itself into knots. The coma issue was especially nightmarish. In some respects, she was glad that Marcus hadn't lingered in that sort of limbo, which would have only given her hope.

"I asked Jax to come over for dinner tonight," Cecilia explained. "But he hasn't written me back."

"He's got a lot on his plate," Nora said quietly.

Cecilia shook her head. "They officially declared the accident wasn't his fault. But I don't know what to think. I've heard rumors about Marcy Coleman that make my ears shiver. Who knows how she was distracting him?"

Nora's jaw dropped. Never had she ever heard anyone blame Marcus for the car accident. It would have chilled her to the bone.

"These girls who leave the island for college are no good at all," Cecilia went on. "Our Jax should date a real island girl, someone without such pretentious plans."

"Jax told me she wants to be a teacher," Nora said, her voice wavering. "And that she wants to teach at a Nantucket school."

Cecilia waved her hand and stood up to disappear into the kitchen. As she poured water into a glass, she babbled on about having heard that Boston University wasn't a very good college and that young women should really go to all-girls colleges, anyway. Nora stood and grabbed her cardigan, unwilling to spend another moment alone with her sister. She loved her, but Cecilia was so needlessly cruel and judgmental sometimes. No wonder Nora had felt so alone over the years.

"Are you leaving?" Cecilia asked with surprise when she returned to the dining room.

"I just remembered that I'm meeting an artist at the shop," Nora said. "But I'll talk to you soon, okay? Keep me updated on Jax."

Nora drove back home in silence, not bothering to turn on the radio. When she entered her house, she drank a glass of water and then grabbed a book, planning to sit in the backyard before the full glory of her garden and escape her anxious mind. But when she stepped out the backdoor, she was surprised to find Jax on his knees in the garden, weeding as tears poured down his cheeks.

"Jax?" Nora's heart lifted.

Jax turned and stood slowly, careful not to stomp on any vegetables as he walked toward her. "Aunt Nora. Hi. I hope it's okay that I came by."

Nora hurried back inside to pour Jax a glass of lemonade, which she handed to him and watched him drink quickly, as though he was very thirsty. She then refilled his glass and led him outside, where they sat quietly for a few moments before she asked him, "How is she?"

Jax raised his shoulders. "The doctors say they just don't know when she's going to wake up."

"Are you able to spend time with her? In the room?"

Jax shifted in his chair. "Her family is always there. I don't know why, but they let me go in every once in a while."

"And Charlie hasn't given you any grief?"

Jax shook his head. "That first night, he looked at me like he wanted to punch me."

Nora clung hard to her glass of water, thinking it might break under the pressure of her hand. *What right did Charlie have to be angry after what he'd done to Marcus?* Then again, she realized that if she could be angry with Charlie, then Charlie could be angry with Jax. But what was the point? Hadn't that anger just made her very sad and alone?

"I didn't want to tell you I was dating Marcy," Jax breathed.

Nora nodded. "I'm sure I didn't make it easy for you."

"It's understandable," Jax said. "What happened to Marcus completely changed your life forever."

"Yes, but..." Nora paused, searching her mind. "Maybe this is obvious to a young man as in tune with himself and his emotions as you are, but I don't think I handled Marcus' death in a healthy way. I completely abandoned my husband. He felt alone in the marriage, so I don't blame him for leaving."

Jax frowned. "You were grieving."

"Yes. I was. And I've allowed myself to continue to grieve for more than thirty years," Nora continued. "But I never should have put pressure on you not to see Marcy Coleman. It's not like you were going to listen to your great-aunt, anyway."

Jax's lips quivered as though he wanted to smile. "I am falling in love with her."

"As you should," Nora said. "Love is a wonderful and magical thing. And everyone deserves to experience it with whomever they choose. My past should not affect your future."

Jax nodded and sipped his lemonade, his face tight with concentration.

"Can I tell you something I've never told anyone?" Nora asked.

"Okay."

"After Marcus died, I didn't touch his bedroom for a very long time," Nora said. "I felt it was a sacred place, as though, just because it remained intact, one day, he would walk back in the door and return to his bedroom as though nothing had happened. But after Jeffrey had gone and I'd felt myself getting older and sadder, I knew I had to do something about that room. More than that, it was getting really dusty, and it started to feel like a cancerous tumor, growing bigger and bigger. So, one morning, probably three years after Marcus died, I began to clear some of the clutter, vacuum, and dust. And I found something on his desk, something that felt so terrible to read at the time."

"What was it?" Jax asked.

"He'd written a to-do list," Nora said. "On it, he wrote: 'Get a degree, get off the island, and make something of yourself.'"

Jax nodded, perplexed.

"It's hard to explain what it was like back then because things have changed so much in just a short time," Nora went on. "But I was pretty sure that after Marcus' graduation, he wanted to marry his high school sweetheart, settle down, and have babies, just as his father and I had done. Instead, Marcus wanted much more than we'd ever given him, and that frightened me. Even if he had lived, I realized, he would have run as far away from me as he could after that.

"I didn't know what to do after I learned that. I got very angry and stayed away from his room for a while. I didn't even go to his grave for over a week! I felt very petty." Nora shook her head at the memory. "But since then, I've learned to be grateful for what I learned that day. Marcus was imaginative and open-hearted. I truly believe he did the best with the time he had."

"Not everyone can say that," Jax said.

"I know," Nora breathed. "I don't think anyone could say that I've used my life well. I've spent so much of it alone in this big house or tending to my garden."

Jax turned to gaze at the rows of vegetables, their green leaves gleaming beneath the sun. "It's a damn good garden," he said.

Nora laughed in spite of herself. "It is, isn't it?" Her heart was in her throat.

After Jax left that afternoon to return to the hospital, there was a knock on Nora's door. Nora rubbed her eyes of tears and hurried to answer it. There, holding a large bouquet of roses, was the man of her dreams, Alan. Behind his glasses, his eyes were red with sorrow, and he seemed as nervous as a younger man on the brink of the rest of his life.

"Nora," Alan began, "I'm sorry to drop by like this. I felt like a stupid phone call or a text wasn't enough."

Nora took the bouquet of flowers wordlessly. Everything felt so crazy. And then, she threw herself into Alan's arms, burrowing her face against his chest.

"I'm sorry I left so quickly the other night," Nora said. "I was so worried about my great-nephew. And the night reminded me so much of the night my son died. I didn't want you to see me like that."

Nora led Alan into her home for the very first time, watching as he sat nervously at the table. She placed the roses in a vase. They were the first flowers anyone had given her in probably thirty-five years.

Outside, clouds descended upon their little island, thickening and darkening. Thunder rolled across the hills, and lightning dissected the sky. Nora jumped at the next bolt, her eyes wide open with fear. Alan stood and wrapped his arms around her, saying, "It's all right."

"You got here right in time," Nora said to him softly, the words taking on several different meanings as the rain began to pelt against the garden leaves, the windowpanes, and the top of the roof. So many years ago, her life had stopped in its tracks, yet Alan had come to rip the door open again and guide her back into the light. It was finally time.

Chapter Eighteen

Spring 1994

Because Jeffrey and Nora hadn't been up to it immediately after Marcus' death, the decision to have a memorial service for Marcus Fuller came from Nantucket High School. Students who'd loved Marcus had contributed hundreds of photographs, donated flowers, and arranged for speeches and songs in his honor. The service was set to begin Saturday afternoon at three, and Charlie dreaded it.

Charlie was now eighteen years old and living with Shawna in a very small apartment not far from the Nantucket Historic District. To make ends meet, Shawna worked as a waitress at a fish restaurant, which required her to scrub herself clean every night after work, as she hated the smell of fish. Charlie had taken a job with his father, who wanted to show him the ropes of his business. Unfortunately, Charlie felt himself butt heads with Roland frequently, in a way that made him ask himself several questions. Again, he was terrified that working too closely with Roland would ultimately tear them apart. Charlie was the kind of guy who wanted to build his own thing, anyway, just like Roland had been when he'd broken away from Grandpa Chuck's business.

On Saturday morning, Charlie awoke to find Shawna in the kitchen with a big pot of coffee and some donuts. She stood and hugged him lovingly, then poured him a mug of coffee and said, "Are you feeling okay?"

Charlie was not feeling okay. All night, he'd tossed and turned with nightmares, seeing Marcus around every corner, beneath murky waters, and even at the top branch of a tree. Sometimes, Marcus screamed at Charlie that it was his fault, that Charlie had murdered him. And sometimes, when Charlie woke up, he believed him. Yes, the driver who hadn't had his lights on was currently in prison for the accident, but to Charlie, he was the one at fault. Charlie had been the one who'd told Marcus he would get him home safe. The night hadn't played out like that at all.

Charlie and Shawna dressed in black and walked to the Nantucket funeral home in a kind of daze. A few blocks before, they happened to run into Evie, who looked much older than eighteen, her hair in long strings down her back. After Marcus' death, she'd fallen apart, telling everyone she'd planned to marry Marcus one day. Charlie had never told anyone what Marcus had told him on that last night: that he had no plans to marry Evie and that he wanted to leave the island and build his own life.

Shawna hugged Evie close and walked along with her, asking her questions about her job at the nail salon and whether she'd considered going to college somewhere, just as a fresh start. Evie answered softly, mostly saying, "I don't know." She didn't look at Charlie at all.

At the funeral home, Charlie stood outside for a while and watched his classmates stream in. Most everyone had remained on the island after graduation to stay near family and uphold the heart of the island, just as Charlie had. A few babies had been born over autumn and winter after surprise late-high school pregnancies. Their eighteen-year-old mothers carried them against their chests as they spoke quietly to other classmates and walked slowly. Shawna greeted the mothers and the babies with wide eyes, hopeful for babies of her own in the future. This terrified yet thrilled Charlie. He knew that having a baby opened you up to the great mysteries of the universe, but it also put you at the mercy of the biggest heartbreaks.

Charlie and Shawna entered the funeral home and kept themselves toward the back, where Charlie hoped he would bleed in with the rest of the crowd. Up front, photos of Marcus hung all over the walls, trying to illustrate the entire seventeen years of his life. And in the first row sat Nora, all in black, her head bent. Several seats to her left sat Jeffrey, her husband, who, it was rumored, had left her for a woman in Providence. As Charlie studied their heads, Jeffrey bent slightly to the right to say something to Nora, but she didn't seem to answer him.

In Charlie's memory, Nora and Jeffrey had been a wonderful couple, the sort that laughed at dinner and teased one another. Now, they acted like strangers.

The memorial service was very long. It seemed that everyone wanted to stand up to tell a story about Marcus, sing a song Marcus had liked, or link themselves to the tragedy. Charlie felt several eyes upon him as though they expected him to head up to the front and say a few words. He was, after all, Marcus' best friend. But Charlie was terrified of what would happen if he went up there. He imagined Nora jumping to her feet and screaming at him, telling him what a monster he was. He wouldn't have known how to disagree with her.

After the service, the president of the student body stood on a chair and announced there was a big dinner planned at the Nantucket High School cafeteria and that everyone was invited. This seemed to excite the class, as now that they'd graduated, they didn't see one another every day, and it was nice, for a moment, to slip back into their old routines.

"Do you want to go?" Shawna asked as they headed out.

"I don't know," Charlie said. "Senior year was a nightmare for me. I was so glad to graduate."

Shawna nodded. "I figured. Why don't we just go home? We can order pizza."

Suddenly, Charlie felt as though someone was staring at him. He turned his head and found his eyes locked onto Nora's as she passed him by, her face stricken and pale. For a moment, he thought this was it, that she would finally unleash all her rage upon him. But instead, Jeffrey stepped between them, extended his hand, and said, "Hi, Charlie. I hope you're well?"

Charlie gaped at Jeffrey's hand as though it was a snake about to attack him. He swallowed and shook Jeffrey's hand, then said, "I heard you left the island."

Jeffrey's face flashed with pain. "I miss Nantucket every day."

"Why don't you come back?"

One corner of Jeffrey's lips curved upward. "If only I could, Charlie." He released Charlie's hand and patted him on the shoulder, then turned back to walk toward the parking lot. Nora remained alone, walking the route back to the house where she now resided by herself.

But that afternoon over pizza, Charlie couldn't help but burst out something he swore he would never repeat. "Marcus wanted to leave the island after graduation. He didn't want to be here."

Shawna set down her slice of pizza. "He told you that?"

Charlie nodded. "I can't help but think it should have been me, you know? Marcus had all these dreams. He wanted things in a way that I don't know how."

Shawna frowned, suddenly angry.

"He was going to go to the city and make a name for himself," Charlie continued. "He didn't want to be chained to the island and follow his father's footsteps."

"What's so bad about being like your father?" Shawna demanded.

Charlie grimaced and sipped his cola.

"Charlie..." Shawna stood and walked around to hug him from behind. "It hurts me when you say it should have been you."

"I know. I'm sorry." Charlie's voice wavered.

"You have dreams, too, Charlie," Shawna said. "We've talked about getting married. About having babies. And you've talked about opening your own business to get out from under your father's shadow."

"Yes, but are those dreams enough?"

Shawna's arms were stiff. "Of course! Those dreams are filled with love. Isn't that enough?"

Although it pained him, Charlie knew Shawna was right. And that night, he began to construct a plan to start his own business; he dared to dream of a big house of his own and two or three children who called him "dad." Bit by bit, the sorrows of the past became a fuel that powered him to a brighter future, as he knew, above everything, he had to make Marcus proud of him. He had to show him that he was willing to fight for his dreams because, for some reason, he'd been spared that night. And life was meant to be lived.

Chapter Nineteen

Present Day

With Marcy in a coma, Grandpa Chuck had decided to stay in Nantucket for the time being. Roland had offered him a room at the Coleman House, and Chuck had accepted, bringing a suitcase along with him. Now, as Charlie walked through the front of the house toward the back porch, he saw Roland and Chuck, son and father, seated beneath the shade of the porch umbrella, drinking coffee as the sun lifted higher in the morning sky. Had Charlie not been deep underwater and tremendously sad, he might have been warmed by the image.

"Morning," Grandpa Chuck said as Charlie stepped out on the porch.

Estelle hurried outside. Her eyes were very small, and she looked as though she hadn't been sleeping. "Did you go home at all last night?" she asked Charlie as she handed him a cup of coffee.

"Naw." Charlie waved his hand. "At some point, it just felt easier to sleep up there."

"I'm sure Shawna hasn't left Marcy's room at all," Estelle said softly.

"It's difficult to get her to go home for a shower and a proper meal," Charlie said. "But I've managed a few times."

"And that boy?" Grandpa Chuck eyed Charlie nervously. "Is he still sniffing around?"

Charlie sighed and dropped into a chair, unsure how to answer questions about Jax. Of course, he still felt a dull anger toward the boy, and Roland, Grandpa Chuck, and many other members of the family shared that anger. But more than that, he recognized that the anger was a detriment to his own healing— and he didn't want to give it much power.

"We've let him sit in the hospital room with her a few times." Charlie sipped his coffee. "Shawna and I don't see any reason to hold a grudge."

Roland and Grandpa Chuck exchanged glances.

"Dad," Charlie interjected, sensing their judgment. "I don't have to tell you how much Nora Fuller has hated me over the years."

Roland couldn't look Charlie in the eye. Beside him, Grandpa Chuck spoke up. "Who is Nora Fuller?"

"You met her last week at Oriana's party," Charlie explained. "She's the mother of my best friend from childhood. His name was Marcus, and he died in a car accident when we were seventeen." Charlie swallowed, then added, his voice wavering, "I was driving."

Grandpa Chuck seemed to look at Charlie with fresh eyes. Charlie realized this was one of the first times he'd ever told this story, as it was just assumed that people knew about it already. It was not an easy truth to say aloud.

"It wasn't your fault," Estelle said softly. "The other driver did a number of years in prison."

"He didn't have his lights on," Roland coughed. "So late at night, driving around the middle of nowhere without his lights!"

Charlie remained quiet, feeling his grandfather's eyes upon him.

"That must have been a terrible time, Charlie," Grandpa Chuck said quietly. "I'm very sorry I wasn't here for you."

Charlie nodded, surprised at how much he'd needed to hear that. "It was a lonely time. But my family and Shawna were my backbone."

"That doesn't mean the grief ever fully goes away," Grandpa Chuck said.

"No. It never did." Charlie sipped his coffee, then added, "I was too much of a fool and a coward to tell my children what happened. I wish I would have if only to explain to them that life doesn't always go as we plan. And that, although I want to appear to be this perfect 'dad of Nantucket,' I'm just a messed-up teenager at heart."

"We're all messed-up teenagers at heart," Grandpa Chuck said. "When I first started the affair, I remember thinking that I finally felt young again. But the truth is, we always feel young and frightened and unsure. I let myself feel romantic about that youth, but it was a way to hide from the fear of it all, too."

After Charlie finished his coffee, he hugged his mother, father, and grandfather and then headed to the grocery to buy a few items for the house. As he walked from the parking lot into the grocery store, the world around him spun and blurred, and he paused for a moment to grab a telephone pole and breathe deeply. It was true that he hadn't slept much at all in the last few days, so he made up his mind to take a taxi to the hospital rather than endanger others on the road.

Inside the grocery store, Charlie filled his basket with crackers, cheese, diet soda, fruits, pre-packaged sandwiches, nuts, chips, and dips. He had a hunch that nobody in his family would bother to eat it at all, but buying it made him feel as though he was providing for them during this difficult time.

At the cash register, a woman Charlie had gone to high school with scanned the products and eyed him nervously.

"We're all pulling for Marcy, you know," she said.

Charlie couldn't make eye contact with her. He was pretty sure he remembered seeing her at Marcus' memorial service all those years ago. She'd probably used the lunch afterward as a fun social time. She'd probably told stories about how well she'd known Marcus, even though Charlie was pretty sure Marcus hadn't known her at all.

Gosh, he felt cruel. The inside of his head was a twisted web. He thanked the woman at the cash register, filled a paper bag with his purchases, and hurried outside to hail a taxi. The taxi driver was quiet throughout the drive, and Charlie gave him a serious tip when they arrived. Empathy was a big part of taxi driving, he thought.

Inside, he found Sheila and her fiancé, Jonathon, in the waiting room with their legs stretched out in front of them. Jax sat in the far corner with big earphones on his ears to block out the world. A moment later, Vince appeared, his hair greasy across his forehead.

"I brought food," Charlie said quietly, placing the bag next to Sheila.

Sheila stood to hug him as Vince explained Shawna was in with Marcy, the doctor had just come in to check her vitals, and she still seemed healthy— just not awake.

"I think she knows we're here," Sheila said. "She can sense it."

"I'm sure you're right," Charlie said.

Charlie urged his children to eat, then walked down the hallway to find his wife. At the window to Marcy's room, he watched as Shawna held Marcy's hand and spoke to her, smiling lightly as though she wanted her voice to be happy and bright. When he entered, Shawna turned to him and said, "And your daddy is here! Say hi to him!"

Charlie smiled and said, "Good morning, Marcy." He sat across from Shawna and took Marcy's other hand.

"We've had a nice morning," Shawna explained. "We listened to a podcast about teaching, which was very informative. And after that, we listened to some of Marcy's favorite songs from high school. I hate to admit it, but I don't know what kind of music she's into these days!"

"At twenty-one, I guess Marcy is experimenting with genres. I was at that age," Charlie said.

"That's not really true," Shawna reminded him. "We had Vince when we were twenty-one. We were experimenting with different diaper brands, not music genres."

Charlie laughed. Privately, they'd agreed to sound happy, to laugh often, and to say Marcy's name frequently as a way to call her back to the world.

"Do you think we had babies too young?" Charlie asked.

"I was baby crazy from an early age. Don't you remember?"

"I remember, all right." Charlie laughed. "I think we did all right, regardless of how young we were. You became a pretty dang successful essayist, and my silly business turns a pretty good profit if I do say so myself."

Shawna laughed, and tears sprung to her eyes. "You and your father just couldn't hack working together. I remember that."

"Lots and lots of fights," Charlie agreed.

Charlie then turned toward Marcy, blinking back tears as he said, "Marcy, I was thinking about a memory I have of you from when you were just a little thing."

"Tell her," Shawna rasped. "I'm sure she'd love to hear it."

"You were probably seven," Charlie continued, "and at the peak of your obsession with Barbies. And although I was your imperfect father, who always seemed to have a work commitment, you were able to talk me into sitting on the floor to play with you."

Across the bed, Shawna stifled a sob.

"You instructed me on which of the Barbies I was allowed to play with," Charlie said. "And we got to work, building a little story together— a collaborative plot about a princess and a cow and a wicked stepmother, something Disney-like that pleased you very much. I was in charge of moving the cow from place to place, and, at one point, I picked up the cow, pointed his nose at yours, and began to speak directly to you as the cow. Oh, your face at that moment! You looked at me like I was insane."

Shawna laughed gently, tears spilling down her cheeks.

"You said, 'Dad, you're not playing right,' as though I'd just broken a Biblical rule," Charlie went on. "And I asked you, 'Why, Marcy?' You told me that, first of all, cows don't speak, and second of all, you, Marcy, weren't a character in the story, and therefore, the cow wouldn't have spoken to you in the first place. I told you I understood, and we carried on. But not long afterward, I picked up the cow again and had the cow ask you a question. Oh, your face! You went beet-red. And instead of speaking directly to me, you addressed the cow and said, 'Mister Cow, I'm not in this!' And your eyes were so big and serious. It took everything I had not to explode with laughter."

Charlie chuckled to himself, remembering the feel of Marcy's toy cow in his hand and the anger on little Marcy's face when he'd broken her rules.

"You were such a strong little thing," Charlie continued, his voice breaking. "Ever since you learned to walk and talk, your mother and I said, 'Uh oh. We're in for trouble.' And we were! You made it very clear that you had a mind of your own. We couldn't tell you to do anything without you demanding the reason behind it. We imagined you as a politician or a lawyer later on and were pleased as punch to learn you wanted to be a teacher. This nation, no, this world, needs teachers like that— teachers willing to stand up for their students. Your mother and I can't wait to come to visit your first classroom next year to watch as you help sculpt the minds of the next generation." Charlie closed his eyes, imagining the scene as though, if he willed it hard enough, it would come true.

Charlie and Shawna remained quiet for a little while, both still holding onto Marcy's hands. After an hour like that, give or take, Shawna raised her chin and said, "Do you think it's time we give Jax a chance?"

Charlie's stomach twisted. "Not yet. Not till later."

Shawna nodded and dropped her head again. A moment later, there was a soft knock on the door, and Vince and Sheila appeared, placing chairs next to their mother and father and sitting there, as a family of five, without spouses or grandchildren or anyone else. It was surreal to Charlie that it being just the five of them had been commonplace for him for many, many years.

"I think her cheeks look pinker," Sheila said, adjusting the blanket slightly over Marcy's shoulder. "I was always so jealous of that skin! Look at the way it glows."

Shawna nodded. "I'm sorry to say you got my complexion, honey. We break out easily."

"Marcy, you hear that?" Sheila's voice broke. She seemed to barely hold onto reality. "Even Mom admits it. Wouldn't you love to gloat about it now?"

Not long afterward, as Shawna and Sheila began to update Marcy on celebrity gossip as a way to keep her involved with the rest of the world, Charlie stood up and went to the bathroom down the hall. Then he purchased a Diet Coke from a vending machine and stood by the large window for a while, watching as the July wind cut through the leaves of the trees that surrounded the parking lot. Recently, the island had been plagued with numerous thunderstorms, and it seemed that that day was no different. The leaves flipped wildly, showing their white underbellies, a sign of approaching rain.

Suddenly, there was the sound of shoes squeaking in the hall, and Charlie turned to find Jax at the corner near the vending machines, his face pale. He looked from Charlie to the vending machines and then out at the rolling clouds that drove across the ocean, ready to attack their little island. For a moment, Charlie just stared at him, imagining all the insults he wanted to hurl. But again, Jax's face echoed Marcus' in such a way that Charlie became tongue-tied. *How could he possibly ridicule this young man when he was so clearly heartbroken?*

Over and over again, Charlie had asked himself: *why me? Why was I saved that night?* And he knew there was no answer to any of his questions. Life had its way with you. It took whatever it wanted and left you to deal with the consequences.

Jax bought a Gatorade from the vending machine, retrieved it, then stood to blink at Charlie through the shadows of the hall. This was the man who'd fallen in love with Charlie's daughter. This was the man Charlie's daughter had chosen to love.

"You can see her soon," Charlie heard himself say.

Jax remained quiet for a moment until he said, "Whenever you're ready," and turned on his heel and made his way back to the waiting area. It took everything Charlie had not to fall to his knees in the hallway and break into sobs, while outside, thunder made the sky sound as if it was being boiled. Charlie prayed that one day, this would only be a nightmarish memory.

Chapter Twenty

I t had been more than thirty years since Nora Fuller had shared a bed with a man. That first night that Alan stayed in Nantucket to be with her, she'd watched him fall easily to sleep beside her, his face calm as the moonlight played across his cheeks and curly hair. For hours, she could do nothing but lay there, praying that when she woke up, he wouldn't be gone.

The next morning, the other side of the bed was empty, which gave her a moment's fright until she smelled the air, which was thick with the scent of bacon. She popped up, smiling from ear to ear, remembering how, as a young girl, her mother always cooked breakfast on Saturday mornings, insisting that Nora, Cecilia, and their father sit together at the dining room table to talk about their weeks and what they wanted to do together as a family that day. Nora had done the same when Marcus was a boy, watching as Marcus and Jeffrey had read the newspaper comic strips, laughing together in a way that had made her heart balloon.

Nora grabbed her robe and hurried downstairs, where

she found Marcus in an apron, a spatula beneath two beautiful fried eggs as he raised them to a plate.

"Morning, sleepyhead!"

Nora laughed. "What on earth are you doing?"

"I thought I'd cook you up something heavenly," Marcus said. "We're between thunderstorms this morning. The first one cut out about thirty minutes ago, but another one is hot on its heels. But look, now." He pointed with the spatula at the backyard, which was drenched in sunlight. "This is the only sunlight we'll have. Look at the vegetables! They're drinking it in."

Nora peered out the window at the vibrant plants, which seemed to have grown twice their height since the rains had come. A moment later, Alan wrapped his arms around her from behind and kissed her neck, inhaling the scent of her. Nora nearly lost her mind at his touch. She turned to face him, closed her eyes, and kissed him with everything she had— grateful that kissing was something that had come back to her, even after so many decades of not doing it at all.

Together, Nora and Alan feasted at the kitchen table as torrential rain began again, pounding against the windowpanes and the back patio. Nora laughed and ate, her soul opening up as Alan told her stories about his sailing adventures, his hiking trips, and his treks across Europe. It seemed Alan had done everything and seen everything there was to see.

When there was a lag in the conversation, Nora returned to a question she'd been dying to ask Alan for a while.

"What's on your mind?" Alan asked, sensing it.

"Oh, it's silly, really. I've just wanted to ask you something."

"Ask away. Nothing is off-limits," Alan told her.

Nora cleaned her hands with her napkin and hoped he wasn't lying. "I was just curious why you and your wife never had children."

Alan's eyes widened. "I do have children."

Nora's jaw dropped. "What? Why hadn't you mentioned them?"

"They don't live close anymore," Alan said sadly. "And I don't see them very much." He leafed through his pocket to find his wallet, from which he removed two photographs, one of a woman in her thirties and another of a woman in her late twenties. "This is Hannah, and this is Lauren."

"Wow," Nora breathed, captivated by them.

"They look like their mother," Alan explained timidly. "They didn't get any of my weird genes."

"You don't have weird genes," Nora said.

"Oh, but I do." Alan removed his glasses to show how thick the lenses were, proof that he was nearly blind.

"Your glasses are charming. You wouldn't be you without them," Nora said.

Alan smiled and slid the photographs back into his wallet, grateful to have revealed this side of himself. "Maybe sometime, we can go out to California to visit them. There's plenty of hiking to do out there if you're interested in that."

It made Nora think about a time a long time ago when Nora and Jeffrey had taken Marcus on a hiking trip through Maine. Marcus had been young yet vibrant, but the weather had been wretched, whipping through their clothes in a way that left them exhausted and freezing for most of the trek.

"You'll have to show me what you like about hiking,"

Nora said softly, surprised that Alan was so open about sharing his life with her.

"Out there between the trees and the mountains, my soul feels quiet and free. There, I'm at peace with everything that happened and everything that's going to happen. It's a sort of meditation on life and everything it gives and everything it takes away," Alan explained.

Nora nodded and sipped her coffee. It almost sounded too good to be true, and yet, with Alan by her side, she had a sense she could believe in anything. Maybe she didn't have to be pessimistic anymore. Maybe there was much more to life.

To Nora's surprise, Alan helped her with the dishes that first morning, then sat with her to do the crossword as she read a book. The rain continued, but it softened to a dull roar that calmed Nora's mind. Once, when it quit for a good thirty minutes, she expected Alan to say he wanted to head back to the Vineyard to "get things done at home" or something, but he didn't. Instead, he said, "What should we cook for dinner?"

Nora knew that Alan wouldn't stay in Nantucket forever— that if they were going to make a relationship work between them, they would have to find a way to compromise. Perhaps eventually, when they'd been together a little while, they would pick one island to stay on. Strangely enough, Nora was open to the idea of moving off Nantucket.

She hoped she wasn't getting ahead of herself.

In fact, that night, as Alan got ready for bed, Nora read an article someone posted on Facebook about a woman who'd married a con artist who'd taken all of her money and run off to South America. The story chilled Nora to the bone, so much so that when Alan came to bed, she looked at him with a stricken expression. Alan laughed and asked, "You're looking at me like I'm a ghost."

"Are you a ghost?" Nora asked.

Alan laughed louder. "I hope not. I can't imagine what unfinished business I have here if so."

Nora shivered, then dropped her gaze. Alan reached over to take her hand, then said solemnly, "Let me know if we're moving too fast. I can sleep on the couch, no problem."

"No," Nora said, surprised at how much she wanted him to stay in bed with her. "I'm just frightened, I guess. I don't want to find out later I was stupid for trusting you."

"I can guarantee you'll find out how stupid I am," Alan joked. "That I've made about a thousand mistakes and plan to make a thousand more. But beyond that, I know for sure that you can trust me. I want to be with you, Nora. I want you to know me, and I want to know you back."

Nora felt woozy from his kindness. Slowly, she leaned her head against his chest and cuddled close to him, listening as the winds rushed across the windows and shook the house.

Throughout this very strange time, Nora could not escape thoughts of Marcy. There was no news of the girl's health besides that she remained in that hospital bed, unconscious. The island mourned her already, speaking sullenly about Marcy at the grocery store or the movie theater or the local bar. "What a pity it is," they said. "She's so young. And she wanted to be a teacher!"

When Nora and Alan went to a local diner for some food the following lunchtime, Nora tuned in to a couple speaking about Marcy at the corner table. They ate Reubens and talked about how dangerous their own teenage lives had been; they said they'd always driven drunk and always stayed up too late. "We were lucky," the woman told her husband softly. "It doesn't seem fair that other kids don't have that luck."

Nora was no longer hungry. Alan, who'd overheard the couple, as well, placed his hand over hers on the table and said, "Do you want to talk about it?"

"I don't know if there's anything left to say."

Alan nodded.

"But..." Nora winced at her own shortcomings, then went on. "I do think I should stop by the hospital. I could bring Jax a sandwich, at least. And maybe, I could say hello to Charlie. And apologize."

"You don't have to do that," Alan told her.

"I do," Nora breathed. "I think it's the only way I can free myself from what happened. I've been clinging to my anger toward Charlie for so many years. It hasn't been fair to him, but it also hasn't been fair to me, either."

Alan drove Nora's car up to the hospital, taking it slow due to the perpetual rain. Tourists rushed from here to there under umbrellas, having picked the wrong week to take their vacations. Nora pitied them, knowing that they'd spent hard-earned money on hotel rooms and rental apartments only to hide away from the rain.

Alan carried Nora's umbrella over them both and brought them safely to the hospital doors, where they shook the umbrella out and then walked in, inhaling the sharp medicine scent permeating through the air. The receptionist gave them instructions on where to go, and they walked quietly to the second floor, Nora gripping the sandwich she'd brought for Jax.

In the waiting room, two of Charlie's children sat, watching a video on one of their phones. Down the long hallway, Shawna leaned against the wall and spoke on her phone, nodding as she listened. Charlie was nowhere in sight.

"You okay?" Alan breathed.

Nora nodded, although she wasn't, and continued toward Marcy's hallway. When she reached it, she stopped in her tracks at the sight of Charlie, who stood at the window outside the room, peering in. His face was captivated. At this moment, Nora remembered him as he'd been so many years ago— a football quarterback on the brink of greatness.

Slowly, Nora walked down the hall, her eyes opening wider as she neared him. When she reached the window to Marcy's room, she followed Charlie's gaze to find her great-nephew, Jax, there beside Marcy's bed. Both of his hands were wrapped around one of Marcy's, and he spoke to her quietly, his eyes urgent. It was impossible to know what Jax told her now as she lay there unconscious beside him. Everything on his face echoed love.

"Charlie?" Nora breathed, surprising herself.

Charlie flinched, then turned, surprised to find her beside him. "Nora?"

Nora pressed her lips into a fine line, searching her heart for any hatred for Charlie. It was gone. "How are you holding up, honey?" Nora asked, her voice breaking.

Charlie sniffed and nodded, on the verge of falling apart. "It's not easy."

"Have the doctors said anything?"

"Nothing new," Charlie said. "We're just in limbo,

praying she'll wake up soon." He nodded toward Jax through the window to add, "Jax has hardly left the hospital."

Nora swallowed. "He told me he's in love with her, you know."

Charlie remained quiet for a moment, his eyes churning with this new information. "When they're kids, you just want them to stay young and curious and happy forever."

Nora nodded, remembering that from her long-ago days with a young and vibrant Marcus.

"But now, I want her to have that," Charlie continued. "Love, I mean. With him, if she wants that." Charlie shook his head, then added, "I know, now, why you hate me. I see it so clearly. I've been allowed to build an entire life. And Marcus..."

Nora's heart seized at the mention of Marcus' name. Suddenly, she reached out to take Charlie's hand, surprising herself. Charlie took it, frowning.

"Listen, Charlie," Nora said. "What happened in 1992 was the single-worst thing that happened in my life. But I know it was the worst thing that happened to you, too. I never should have demonized you for what happened. It wasn't your fault. Yes, you were lucky to walk out of this very hospital and go on to live a wonderful life. But it just as easily could have gone the other way. That's fate. And as humans, we're left to deal with that."

Charlie set his jaw. "I'm not a big fan of fate."

"Don't be like me, Charlie," Nora breathed. "Don't live your life filled with anger. My anger robbed me of decades of happiness. I shoved my husband as far away from me as I could. And now, I find myself at sixty-seven, with not too many years ahead of me. I regret living in darkness for so long. Marcus wouldn't have wanted that."

On the other side of the mirror, Jax flinched up and locked eyes with Nora. He squeezed Marcy's hand gently, then stood and walked ponderously toward the door that separated Charlie and Nora from the twenty-something couple. He then stepped out of the room, closed the door behind him, and placed his back against the wood. His legs shook beneath him.

"Jax, you need to eat something," Nora said, remembering the sandwich still in her hand. She pressed it into his hands, trying to smile at him, but the devastation and guilt in his eyes made it very difficult. It had been so long since Marcy had been awake now. Even those who loved her most had begun to lose hope. "Please, Jax. Please. Eat."

Nora felt herself entering into a mothering autopilot. Quickly, she led Jax down the hallway to a set of chairs nearest the window. There, she sat next to Jax and unwrapped his sandwich. Alan followed after her, sitting next to her with his hand resting assuredly on her shoulder. This was a level of support Nora had never known.

Chapter Twenty One

Charlie had entered a state of delirium. It had been days since he'd slept, days since he'd had a proper meal, and he staggered down the hospital hallway, his eyes glazed. When he reached the waiting area, he clung to the edge of a chair and tried to focus on his breathing but soon felt himself collapse to his knees.

"Charlie?" Shawna's voice barely reached him. It was as though it came from the far end of a very long auditorium. "Charlie?" Suddenly, her hands were on his shoulders, and she was calling for someone to bring water. A moment later, someone handed him a bottle of water, and Charlie dropped his head back and drank. The water was so cold, and his tongue felt numb against it, but as he drank, his vision slowly returned, and his thoughts sped up, and he was able, finally, to muster, "Thank you."

Charlie shrugged into a chair as Shawna and Sheila spoke quietly in the way that women do when they've made a decision without you. Charlie remembered it well from childhood when his mother had spoken quietly to

Nora about Marcus and Charlie, about whether they should get them to bed. Suddenly, Shawna's gorgeous face hovered just a few inches from his, and she whispered, "Charlie? It's late. I think we should go home and get some sleep tonight."

Charlie stuttered with disbelief. "We can't."

"We have to keep ourselves healthy, baby," Shawna told him. "We have to go home, eat a real dinner, and rest."

Downstairs, Shawna called a cab, and as they waited, she explained that Sheila and Vince would be at the hospital all night and that Marcy would have them there if she woke up. Charlie nodded, grateful to his children for their constant love.

The taxi ride home was a blur. Charlie watched Shawna open the front door of the house, then followed her inside, where she announced the pizza would be there in just five minutes. She'd ordered his favorite— meat lover's, which she hadn't allowed him to have since his cholesterol reading had jumped off the charts. At the time, she'd said, "I want you around for a long time, Charlie. Lay off the meat."

But Shawna understood then that they needed to eat something, anything, even though their sorrow told them not to. When the pizza arrived, they turned on the television to a movie they'd seen maybe fifty times, *Airplane*, which they watched sullenly as they ate. Charlie knew every joke by heart, but he couldn't laugh. Still, a comedy in times like these was better than most things.

"Did everything go okay with Nora today?" Shawna asked as they got ready for bed a little later.

"She was very kind." Charlie was quiet for a moment

as he slipped under the covers. "She said she wished she wouldn't have wasted her life."

"That's sad," Shawna breathed.

Still, Charlie knew that if he and Shawna lost their daughter, their grief would be insurmountable. He prayed their love was strong enough to get them through.

"Sheila was wondering if she should postpone the wedding," Shawna said in the dark.

"We shouldn't make any rash decisions."

"She doesn't feel like planning the wedding anymore," Shawna explained.

Charlie was quiet. In his mind, there could be no wedding in their family without Marcy there. He knew Sheila felt the same.

Although it came as a surprise because Charlie was so exhausted, he soon fell into a deep and nightmarish sleep. In it, all the usual players of his nightmares came out. There he was, a young and arrogant jock of seventeen, playing football with his teammates. Many of the players on the opposite team had zombie faces, and they looked at him hungrily, like they wanted to eat him. And then, Marcus was there, just as friendly and handsome as he had been in 1992, and he said, "Don't pay any attention to them. They're dead." Charlie laughed at that, really laughed in a way that made him keel over. They decided to bail on the game, sensing it wasn't fair to play a team like that, and they wandered through a sun-dappled Nantucket, swapping jokes and eating ice cream cones. Finally, toward the end of the dream, Marcus placed his hand on Charlie's shoulder and said, "Man, I don't want to sound cheesy. But you've built a dang good life for yourself. Shawna is just about the sweetest woman in the world, and your children are wonderful, intelligent, and very kind. The thing is, nobody deserves this as much as you, Charlie Coleman. Nobody."

Suddenly, Charlie erupted from his bed, sweat bleeding through his t-shirt. He gasped for breath, his hands on his chest. Beside him, Shawna rolled over and rubbed his leg, cooing, "Are you all right, baby? Was it another nightmare?"

"No," Charlie breathed as he dropped back down onto his pillow. "It wasn't a nightmare this time." But how could he explain how he'd felt with Marcus beside him? It had been a sort of time travel, allowing him the space to pal around with his best buddy for the first time in decades.

Charlie rolled over to check the time on his phone. It was just past four in the morning, and the night sky was still inky black. For some reason, he was now wide awake and unwilling to go back to sleep. His thoughts had returned purposefully to Marcy, and he felt suddenly, madly needed at the hospital. He couldn't wait around the house a moment later.

"I think we should go back up," Charlie said through the dark.

Shawna's voice was clear, as though she'd been awake a while. "Are you sure?"

"I can't get back to sleep."

"Neither can I."

Quickly, Charlie and Shawna showered and dressed, then grabbed the keys to head back to the hospital. On the drive, the island was completely dead, with a few remaining lights that were dim and few and far between.

"I texted Sheila that we're coming back," Shawna said. "But she hasn't read it yet."

"Maybe she fell asleep."

"Maybe. But she always keeps the sound on at night," Shawna said. "It's weird."

Charlie parked the car in the empty parking lot and led Shawna toward the front door, where a guard waved them in, recognizing them. They then took the familiar route to the second floor to find the waiting room empty. Down the hall was a flurry of activity, the sound of rushing feet. *What was going on?*

Charlie and Shawna locked eyes, then rushed around the corner to find Marcy's hospital door wide open. A nurse breezed out, her sneakers squeaking on the linoleum. Charlie broke into a run, both terrified and ecstatic at once. And when he reached the doorway, gasping for breath, he peered into the room to find Sheila and Vince on either side of Marcy, who was glowing beneath hospital lights. Her eyes were open.

"Marcy!" Charlie cried.

Shawna reached the doorway and gasped, and together, they walked toward Marcy's bed, where both Sheila and Vince stuttered to explain what had happened.

"Vince fell asleep around two," Sheila began, "and I was out around three, but my hand was still on Marcy's hand. And sometime after that, I felt her fingers flinching, and I woke up to find her looking at me!"

Marcy continued to peer at the four of them curiously, her eyes only half-open. The doctor had said that when and if she did wake up, talking would be difficult, as would moving her upper body.

"How did you know to come now?" Sheila asked Charlie.

Charlie stuttered with disbelief. He collapsed in the chair beside Vince and took his daughter's hand in his, whispering, "You're safe, Marcy. We're all here. Mom and Dad and Vince and Sheila. And we'll make sure nothing bad happens to you. Okay?"

The nurse returned with the doctor, who greeted everyone and explained they would need to conduct a number of tests. He would give them a few more minutes in the room with Marcy, and after that, only one person could remain for the tests. It was already decided that it would be Shawna, her mother.

"She can hear us?" Charlie asked the doctor before he left.

"She can," the doctor said. "Talk to her as much as you can right now. It's a way to bring her back to the world, bit by bit."

Charlie, Shawna, Sheila, and Vince did as they were told. They swapped stories from years ago, teased Marcy about things she'd done as a child, and spoke about the gorgeous dinners they would prepare for her when she got out of there. Charlie confessed that he'd eaten a meat lover's pizza but that he didn't regret a single bite. There wasn't a dry eye in the room, and, if Charlie wasn't mistaken, he felt Marcy acknowledge everything they said, almost as though she wanted to laugh but couldn't.

The doctor kicked them out shortly afterward. Shawna, Vince, and Sheila gathered in the waiting room and whispered excitedly, relishing the morning and all its miracles. It was just past six, and Charlie was wired as though he'd drunk several cups of coffee. Unable to sit still, he wandered the hallways of the hospital, praying the doctor would reveal even more good news very soon.

Not long into his walk, Charlie turned the corner to find Jax with his back up against the wall and his legs out in front of him. He slept fitfully, his face flinching. If

Charlie wasn't mistaken, Jax seemed to be in the midst of a terrible nightmare. Quickly, Charlie dropped down to place his hands on Jax's shoulders and wake him up. When Jax's eyes opened, he sputtered with confusion, then said, "I'm sorry. Is it okay that I'm sleeping here?"

Charlie smiled, then stepped back. He no longer felt anything like anger toward this young man. "She woke up." He said it simply, knowing they were words that would change Jax's life forever.

Jax bolted to his feet. "She what?"

"She woke up," Charlie repeated. "About an hour ago. They're performing some tests to make sure she's all right."

Jax tore his fingers through his hair, at a loss. "I need to see her," he said. "I need to tell her how sorry I am."

"Jax, no," Charlie said. "It wasn't your fault. Don't beat yourself up. Don't let it consume you." He swallowed, then added, "We've been given a gift today. Let's just celebrate. Okay?"

Jax nodded, then excused himself to clean himself up in the bathroom, and Charlie returned to the waiting room, where morning light spilled through the windows. Sheila cried on the phone to Jonathon about what they'd seen. A few minutes later, Jonathon arrived with a big box of donuts and enough coffee to go around, and he sat and again listened to the play-by-play of Marcy's awakening. Charlie ate a donut filled with caramel cream and drank coffee and eyed the horizon, waiting for one of the island's storms to fill the sky. But miraculously, it seemed they would be spared of storms that morning. Perhaps there would be nothing but blue skies ahead.

Chapter Twenty Two

I t was now the end of July. Nora woke at her home a little past seven and reached for her phone to text Alan, "Good morning." He'd returned to Martha's Vineyard to care for his garden, see some of his friends, and spend some time on his boat, but they had plans that upcoming weekend. He'd invited her to a "re-do" of the party Oriana had had a couple of weeks back— the one that had been abruptly halted by Jax and Marcy's accident. This time, Alan told her, the party was being held in Nantucket at a beautiful home called The Jessabelle House. Nora had heard of it and had always longed to experience its beauty. She could hardly believe she was invited, let alone that she actually planned to join in on a Coleman Party. But, as she'd heard many times over the years, things changed. Now, things were finally changing for her.

Yesterday morning, Jax had called Nora from the hospital to tell her Marcy had woken up. His voice had shimmered with love and hope, and Nora had listened, her own heart widening with his happiness. After they'd hung up, she'd cried for over an hour. When she'd cried herself out, she'd felt so calm and at peace that she'd fallen asleep and slept for eleven hours. It was as though something in her had healed.

Now, Nora showered, dried her hair, and drove to the flower shop to purchase fertilizer and fresh plants. Due to the frequent storms, Marcus' grave was a mess, and it was up to her to fix it. She would always serve as his gardener. She would always watch over him.

Marcus' grave was fifteen rows in and thirty-eight rows to the left of the large fence that surrounded the old cemetery. Nora's parents had been buried on the other side of the cemetery, near their own families, but by the time Marcus had passed away, there hadn't been space over there.

The gravestone itself was regal and rounded, with a bit of detail outlining "Marcus Fuller: April 12, 1975-September 19, 1992." The flowers were forlorn, drooping after too much rain, and Nora dropped to her knees in front of them and tugged them gently from the soil, grateful to replace them again. As she worked, she spoke to Marcus, updating him on the events of the island, including Marcy's recent coma.

"They say it'll take her a while to relearn to walk again," she said, "But Jax says he's going to take her everywhere he goes, no matter what. Isn't that the sweetest thing you've ever heard? I think that boy has a lot of you in him, Marcus. You always cared for people so much, especially your friend, Charlie."

It had been a long time since Nora had seen Marcus' high school girlfriend, Evie, out and about. Not long after graduation, Evie had met another guy, a tourist, and she'd had a few babies. It was rumored she'd gotten divorced and taken her kids off the island to live with another guy, someone who was apparently a lot nicer than the first husband. Nora wondered what Evie thought of Marcus now, so many years after his death. Probably, she thought of him fondly as the first boy she'd ever loved.

As Nora worked, a shadow passed over her hands, and she turned quickly to find an old man walking down the aisle between the graves. At first, she didn't recognize him, and she smiled gently and nodded before returning to her work. But a moment later, the man paused behind her, watching her, and Nora grew agitated. *Didn't he know this was a private and sacred space?*

Nora turned back to glare at the man, hoping he would get a hint. But when she peered into his eyes, a shiver of recognition went up her spine, and she heard herself wheeze. "Jeffrey?"

Jeffrey was now nearly seventy years old, just as she was. The photographs she'd recently seen on social media were a few years old, and his gray hair had become silver since then. He used a cane, which he leaned on now as he looked down at her, the first woman he'd ever loved. In truth, Nora had never doubted Jeffrey's love for her, not even when he'd left.

"Nora Moore, as I live and breathe," he said, using her maiden name.

Nora stood on creaking legs and shook her hands of soil. "I can't believe it's you."

Jeffrey nodded toward the grave. "It had been too long since I'd come to see him."

Nora stepped to the side to allow Jeffrey an easier path toward the grave. "The flowers look nice."

"They needed a touch-up. We've had so many storms," Nora explained.

Love Runs Deep

For a moment, Jeffrey studied the grave, and then, he bent down and touched the top of the stone. Nora remembered so many years ago when Jeffrey had bent to lift a baby Marcus to his chest and cradle him close. Even back then, Jeffrey had been the sort of father they wrote books about and doted on their baby, ensuring that Nora had plenty of time to herself. Her friends back then had envied her, saying their husbands "never helped."

"How are you doing, kid?" Jeffrey said, his smile endearing. "I've missed you, you know. I think of you every time the Minnesota Twins play ball. That was the last team we watched win the World Series, if you remember. 1991."

Nora's throat swelled.

"Things are okay," Jeffrey explained to Marcus. "Providence is no Nantucket, but I've had a fine life there. When I look in the mirror, I see an old man, which is a strange thing. And I so often wonder what you would have been like now, at age forty-eight already. Wow." He shook his head. "Your mom and I had you when we were just kids ourselves. You taught us almost everything we knew about life — and you even taught us everything there was to know about death. We love you, kid. So much."

Nora still couldn't believe it was Jeffrey before her. For many years, she'd tricked herself into believing that Jeffrey no longer thought of Marcus at all, that he'd moved on to his new family, his new children, and his grandchildren as a way to delete Nora and Marcus from his mind. She now understood how wrong she was.

A half-hour later, Nora and Jeffrey sat at a diner together with cups of coffee, eggs, bacon, and toast.

175

They'd always been breakfast fans, and some things never changed.

"So, tell me everything," Jeffrey said, leaning against the table and smiling at her. "You look good. Really good."

Nora blushed and sipped her coffee. "I'm better than I've been in a long time."

Jeffrey's eyes glinted with curiosity. "You met a man."

Nora laughed, surprised at Jeffrey's openness. "How do you know?"

"I can see it. You're in love. You look just like..." Jeffrey paused, stuttered, then went on. "You look just like you did when you fell in love with me."

Nora's heart shattered at the thought. "I'm a bit more wrinkled than I was then."

"Naw. The same girl is there," Jeffrey assured her. "She's just done a bit of living since then, that's all."

Nora dropped his gaze, overwhelmed at how kind he was.

"Tell me. Is he good to you?" Jeffrey asked.

Nora nodded. "He's really good."

"I'm sure he's not good enough. But I don't think anyone ever could be."

"Jeffrey, stop that," Nora teased with a smile. "And your wife? How is she?"

Jeffrey waved a hand. "We got divorced last year."

"Oh no." A wave of sorrow passed over Nora. She hadn't expected this.

"It's not a big deal," Jeffrey explained. "She's a great woman, and we gave each other many, many good years. But we just couldn't stand to live with each other anymore. It happens."

"It happens," Nora repeated.

"Whether I like it or not, it's been home for the past

thirty years," Jeffrey said. "My children live there, and my grandchildren. And besides. The dating pool is a bit bigger than in Nantucket." He winked to make Nora laugh again.

"I imagine so," Nora said. "I met my guy in Martha's Vineyard."

"You betrayed the island!" Jeffrey joked.

"It's actually beautiful over there," Nora said thoughtfully. "I wouldn't mind making the move."

Jeffrey leaned back in his booth, shock marring his face. "Nora Moore, making changes. I love to see it."

"It was about time," Nora said. "Did you regret leaving the island?"

"Yes. I regretted it. I spent most of the first few years twisted up in nightmares about what happened," Jeffrey answered honestly, which surprised Nora. "But after that, I fell into my life a little bit— I relaxed. The nightmares never went away, of course. But I learned to carry them."

Nora sighed. "My nightmares never went away, either."

"You and I should really meet to see Marcus more often," Jeffrey said. "We went way too long without talking. I blame myself for that."

"No. I was mentally checked out. I could hardly maintain my friendships here, let alone with you."

"I knew that better than most," Jeffrey said. "And I should have pushed it."

"It doesn't matter, now," Nora told him, her chin raised.

Jeffrey studied her, and in his face, Nora could still find the love he'd had for her on their wedding day. It was remarkable it hadn't gone away.

"Tell me you'll meet me here on his birthday," Jeffrey

said. "Even if you've left this island for that other one to the west."

"It sounds like a plan to me," Nora said.

Jeffrey insisted on paying and then walked Nora out to the parking lot, where they'd parked side-by-side. Nora had a strange vision of them being this age in another reality— having lived out the previous thirty years side-by-side instead of as strangers. But maybe that was wrong. Maybe they never could be strangers, not to one another.

Chapter Twenty-Three

I t was rare that Charlie was the only one up at the hospital. It was a gorgeous summer day, and for a change of scenery, Sheila and Jonathon had gone for a sail, grateful to experience the world outside the hospital again after so much time within its halls. Shawna was at home, preparing Marcy's bedroom for her return, which was set for tomorrow, and Jax had to return to his job at the restaurant, which had miraculously not fired him after his insistence on staying at the hospital for so much of the past week and a half. Even Estelle had just left, citing a migraine. She'd kissed Marcy on the cheek adoringly, whispering, "We can't wait to celebrate your return home," before she floated down the hallway.

Charlie sat in the hospital chair beside Marcy's bed. Marcy was upright, her hair shining down her shoulders after Sheila's recent attention to it— a "hairstyling event" that had taken the better part of that morning. Marcy held the remote control for the hospital television, which Jax had connected to her laptop so that she could watch her favorite TV shows. Lucky for Charlie, Marcy opted for

something he had always liked back in the old days—
Seinfeld.

"I love this one," Marcy said brightly as Kramer burst
into Jerry's apartment to talk about his new adventures in
owning a hot tub.

Charlie chuckled at Kramer's manic face. "Do other
kids your age watch *Seinfeld*?"

"Some do," Marcy said. "But not many."

Charlie eyed his daughter. "Why do you think you
like it so much?"

"I remember watching it as a kid with you," Marcy
explained simply, then giggled again, her eyes on the
screen.

Charlie said a small prayer of thanks for this moment
of "normal." During Marcy's coma, he would have done
anything to sit with her and watch a sitcom episode for
the thousandth time. These were the magical moments,
he knew.

But something was on Charlie's chest— something
extremely heavy that he needed to help Marcy
understand.

"You know, back in high school, I used to watch this
show with my best friend," Charlie began tentatively.

Marcy turned, her face curious. Probably, Charlie
had never used the term "best friend" before, not with
her, anyway.

"We couldn't wait for it to be on," Charlie went on,
"and we always quoted the episodes at each other afterward, trying to remember as many lines as we could. At
Nantucket High, that was cultural currency."

Marcy chuckled. "You were the quarterback. I'm sure
everything you said was gold."

Charlie raised his shoulder, remembering only a small

fraction of the popularity he'd once enjoyed. "Popularity comes and goes."

"I know that," Marcy reminded him. "Once I got to Boston U, I realized all high school stories hadn't followed me there. But that was a good thing for me. I wasn't exactly the most popular girl in school." She laughed her twinkling laugh.

"I don't remember it like that. It seemed like you had so many friends."

"I did," Marcy said. "But we weren't cheerleaders or football players or gymnasts or any of the popular people. We were band nerds and readers and..."

"I guess you're forgetting that I dated your mom in high school," Charlie interjected. "She hated the concept of popularity. I think that's why I wanted to be with her so badly."

Marcy looked stoic. "I always wondered why the great football quarterback Charlie Coleman didn't want to be with the cheer captain or something."

"Are you kidding? I was head over heels for your mother. She was the smartest girl in school, and she could talk in circles around me. Sometimes, when she jumped on a scientific theory, she would talk about it obsessively until I had to beg her to stop." Charlie smiled to himself, remembering Shawna as a teenage girl. She'd burned so brightly. She still did.

Marcy smiled, leaning closer. The deep cuts on her face had healed a great deal, leaving pink and white slices around her chin and cheeks. "Who was this best friend of yours?"

Charlie's throat tightened. "I met my best friend, Marcus, when I was in kindergarten. After that, we were inseparable, basically like brothers. Everything one of us did, the other had to do, too. When I started dating your mother, Marcus started dating Evie so that we could go on double dates. And he was even the running back on the football team.

"But everything in our lives changed when we were seventeen," Charlie went on, his voice breaking. "We went to a beach party, an area I'm sure you know well. There was drinking. If my memory serves me correctly, I only had two beers early on in the evening, and then I quit. I was more responsible than most at that age. Marcus always begged me to drink more, to keep the night going." Charlie's throat threatened to close. "Around two, your mother, Marcus' girlfriend, Marcus, and I got into my car and drove away from the party. I dropped off the girls at home, and then Marcus and I started one of our classic night chats, one that got into philosophical questions about where we wanted our lives to go. I was wrapped up in it, probably distracted. And when I turned the corner..."

Charlie paused to trace his teeth with his tongue. Gosh, this was harder than he'd thought it would be. Before him, Marcy remained speechless, her eyes enormous.

"There was a truck there," Charlie sputtered. "Without its lights on. And we smashed into it head-on. I don't remember anything for a little while after that. When I came to, I was in the ambulance, and then, at the hospital, I was examined and left in a hospital bed. Nobody told me what was happening to Marcus. The next morning, I was able to walk out of that hospital with my parents, but Marcus... He died."

Marcy's eyes shimmered with tears. "Dad..." She stuttered. "Why didn't you ever tell me this story?"

Charlie shook his head. "I was so ashamed of what I'd done."

Marcy reached out to take Charlie's hand. In her face, Charlie saw the wisdom of a woman who knew the ways of the world and how much it could rip you apart.

"It wasn't your fault," Marcy breathed.

"That doesn't seem to matter," Charlie admitted. "I carry that grief around with me every single day, and I'll probably continue until the day I die."

Marcy remained silent for a moment. "This must have been a terrible reminder of that time."

"Yes. But in this case, the story turned out much differently." He closed his eyes, then added, "My best friend's mother was Nora Fuller. Nora's sister is Jax's grandmother, Cecilia."

Marcy's lips formed a circle. She looked mystified. Charlie then reached into his pocket to retrieve an old photograph of himself and Marcus, taken that very last summer before everything changed forever. In it, Marcus had his arm slung around Charlie's shoulder, and their smiles were enormous. They looked like young men on the brink of taking over the world.

"Wow," Marcy breathed, taking the photograph. "He really looks so much like Jax."

"Yes. He does."

Marcy bit her lower lip. "Is this why you were so weird about Jax when you found out we were dating?"

"Guilty," Charlie admitted. "Nora wasn't handling it well, either. But I think we were both just running away from the ghosts of our past without considering the happiness you'd both found here in the future." He paused for a moment, then added, "And you know how much I hate to admit it when I'm wrong."

Marcy laughed gently and passed the photograph back to Charlie. "Jax told me you've been really kind to him lately."

Charlie shrugged. "He hardly left the hospital. It showed me what kind of man he is. And isn't that exactly the kind of man I should want you to be with?"

"Uh oh. My father likes my boyfriend," Marcy said, wrinkling her nose. "Most girls would turn and run. Not that I can run right now." Marcy gestured at her legs, one of which was broken.

"You'll be all healed up in no time," Charlie insisted. "We're going to help you through this. Heck, the doctor said that if you want to go back to school in September, we can arrange everything."

Marcy nodded, her eyes widening. After a long pause, she said, "I think Jax might come with me to help out."

Charlie's heart lifted. In truth, he'd been terrified to take Marcy back to Boston. He'd imagined her on crutches, hurrying to class, nearly tumbling to the ground. He'd imagined her taking the bus, barely able to clomp up the bus steps. But with Jax there, there would be someone to guide her and someone to ensure she was safe until she returned home at night.

"He's even thinking about taking a few college courses," Marcy continued. "His mom's a nervous wreck about him leaving, but he says he wants to try leaving the island again. At least until we come back." Marcy set her jaw. "I told him I'm set on getting a job at a Nantucket school next year. He says one year off the island should be enough for him."

Charlie's heart opened at his daughter's beautiful plans. He still remembered so long ago when he and Shawna had sat at their kitchen table in their dinky apart-

184

ment to discuss the next steps of their life. It had felt like playing a board game, deciding the best strategy to get to the end of the board with the most points.

"You'll let me know if I can help you and Jax with anything, won't you?" Charlie asked quietly.

Marcy smiled a smile that reminded Charlie so much of Shawna when she'd been twenty-one. "You'll always be the first person we call, Daddy," Marcy said. "We know you have our back in everything we do."

Chapter Twenty-Four

1995

Charlie and Shawna talked about it extensively: when it came down to it, at their wedding, they didn't want to accept any money from the Colemans. To them, the flashy pomp and circumstance of all that Coleman money took away from the true purpose of the wedding itself. They wanted simplicity. They wanted their love to be the only thing that mattered.

When Charlie explained this to Roland about six months before the wedding was set, Roland sat with this news very quietly. He then said, "You're just like me. I never wanted anything to do with my father or his money."

To this, Charlie stuttered, "That's not true. Unlike you and Grandpa, I still want us to be close like a father and son should be. I want us to go for beers in the evening and talk about baseball. I don't want us to hate each other in ten years." He paused contemplatively, then opened his mouth to say that he was ready to stop working with his father, period. It was time he stepped out on his own to build his own business. He planned to operate in windows and doors, which was a business adjacent to Roland's own, which necessitated that they work together often. But because Charlie would be his own boss, instead of Roland, they wouldn't butt heads as often. They would be allowed to build a prosperous and healthy relationship.

As Roland took in this news, he turned to gaze out across the rolling hills and beach along the edge of the Coleman House, where Charlie had grown up. "You're a real man, now, Charlie," Roland said to the wind and the sun and the water. "I'm very proud of you."

But in most ways, Charlie didn't feel like a "real man." He was frightened, frequently awake all night after nightmares, and he was often plagued with the belief that he should have been the one to die in the car accident, not Marcus. Once, he read a newspaper article about a local therapist in Nantucket, and Charlie contemplated giving the therapist a call. But a moment later, he was able to talk himself out of it, telling himself that Coleman men and women didn't go to therapy.

About a week before Charlie's wedding to Shawna, a friend from the football team organized a bachelor party. Six guys Charlie knew well took him out sailing, then to dinner, and then to a few bars around Nantucket. One of them, Jeremy Farley, had been in his own car accident by that time, which had destroyed his chances of getting off the island to play professional football. His high school girlfriend, Alana, had left him to run off to the city to become a model, and Jeremy's life seemed grim.

After Jeremy's accident after the beach party, several Nantucket parents cracked down on the beach parties.

"Too many accidents. Too many deaths" had been their mantra. For a little while, a few adults lingered at the edge of the beach parties, taking drunk high schoolers home to ensure they made it safely. Charlie was grateful for this. He felt how everyone did: that high schoolers were inherently reckless and that they were always going to find a way to get their hands on some alcohol. It was better to guide them home safely rather than demonize them for their decisions.

Still, Charlie often reminded himself that he hadn't been drunk on the night of Marcus' death. But it wasn't like he wanted to go around explaining that to everyone all the time. Probably a lot of them didn't believe him, anyway.

On the night of Charlie's bachelor party, he gazed around the table at the six guys who'd decided to take him out. He'd known them for years at this point. They'd shared a textured mix of experiences. Still, his heart shattered at the thought that his best friend in the world was missing. He should have been there.

Perhaps by now, Marcus would have still been at university— in New York or California or wherever the heck else he'd planned. Perhaps he would have traveled home for Charlie's wedding, bringing with him that reckless smile and that big heart. Perhaps he would have made a speech that showed the depths of his love both for Charlie and the island, the place and person he'd left behind. Perhaps, after Charlie had had kids, he would have sent photographs in the mail to Marcus or called him to talk about the banal moments in his life. Perhaps they would have had things to talk about. Perhaps they wouldn't have.

The night before the wedding, Shawna opted to stay

with her parents while Charlie slept at their apartment alone. That night, as Charlie tossed and turned in bed, the phone rang, and he answered it to hear Shawna's sweet voice on the other end.

"I couldn't fall asleep," she said.

"Neither could I."

Shawna's laugh twinkled through the phone. "I have something to tell you, and I don't think I can wait till tomorrow."

"Tomorrow is supposed to be our wedding day, you know. If you plan on leaving me, you should just do it now."

"You charmer," Shawna said sarcastically.

There was a very long, heavy pause. Charlie sat up in bed, a hunch smacking him over the side of the head. "You're not. Are you?"

Shawna laughed again. "I am."

Charlie's head swam with confusion. He jumped out of bed and began to pace as sweat pooled from his armpits. "You took a test?"

"I bought one this afternoon," Shawna explained. "I couldn't wait."

"Shawna!" Charlie stopped, his eyes on the dark window. Normally, the view out of it was just of the parking lot and a dying tree. "Shawna, we need to get a bigger house!"

"I suppose we do!" Shawna sounded on the verge of tears, so Charlie let his fall, too.

"Let me come pick you up," Charlie said.

"Oh, I don't know. My parents might freak out if I'm not here in the morning."

"Shawna! We're going to have a baby! I want to see you! I can't wait!"

"Well. All right, then. When you put it that way, I suppose I can't refuse."

Charlie drove very slowly all the way to Shawna's, recognizing that now, he was a father, and his life was worth much more, if only because he had to protect someone new. Shawna was waiting for him on the front porch, smiling that big smile of hers. He stepped out and spread his arms wide, and she ran into them, quivering with tears and laughter.

Finally, in one another's arms, they were able to sleep that night. In fact, they slept so deeply that they went straight through their alarm and woke up much too late. Shawna yelped and said, "Charlie! We're getting married today!" She then hurried to the phone to call her mother, who was, in fact, freaking out because Marcy was missing. As Charlie hurried to shower, Shawna calmed her mother down, telling her that she would be up at the church soon and asked if her mother could bring her makeup and her dress.

At the front of that church at exactly two-thirty that afternoon, Charlie smiled a foolish smile and watched the woman who'd once been his teenage girlfriend (all those years ago when he'd decided to ask her to go get ice cream with him) walk toward him in the most beautiful cheap dress she could find. Later, Shawna would call it "my dime store wedding dress" with fondness. To them, they didn't need anything else— not money or finery or the best champagne.

On Charlie's side of the aisle sat Roland, Estelle, Samantha, Hilary, and Great-Aunt Jessabelle, all dressed to the nines and looking up at him with expectation. Beside him, no groomsmen stood. Without Marcus there, Charlie hadn't wanted any.

The ceremony happened very quickly. The minister read the appropriate scriptures, asked for the rings, and demanded that Charlie and Shawna repeat words that millions and millions of other loving couples had said before. Charlie had to hope— no, he had to believe that his and Shawna's love was much stronger than all the loves that had come before. He planned to build the foundation of his life around that love. He knew, with Shawna by his side, nothing could truly go wrong again.

Chapter Twenty-Five

Nora waited for Alan at the Nantucket Harbor. She wore a floral dress, a summer hat, and the brightest red lipstick she could find, and as she stood along the railing with her eyes to the opening of the harbor, several tourists eyed her, smiling curiously, as though she was a sight to see. A moment later, Nora realized she'd been smiling at them, first, as though her happiness flowed through her and spilled out. She laughed to herself, realizing Jeffrey was right. She was falling in love with Alan. She just couldn't stop herself from feeling everything at once.

It was the first week of August, and already Nora could smell the edge of summer creeping toward them. There was fear in many tourists' eyes as they clung to their final, bright month of summer, praying that the heat and the beauty would go on forever. But to Nora, she welcomed autumn and winter. She pictured herself and Alan in front of fireplaces, eating warm stews, and watching old movies. She pictured coziness fit for a Hallmark movie.

For many years, Nora hadn't allowed herself to watch romance movies, as the sight of people falling in love on screen so easily had made her wonder what the heck was wrong with her. But last night, as she'd texted Alan from her couch, she'd put on *When Harry Met Sally* and wept through the many years of Sally and Harry trying to figure themselves and each other out. Nora felt that she was finally figuring herself out, too.

Alan's sailboat appeared in the harbor, and Nora stood at the railing and waved at him, feeling like the ancient Nantucket wives who'd awaited their whaling husbands to come home after campaigns of up to five years. How had they been able to stand it? Probably, the husband who'd come home to their beds hadn't been the same husband who'd left five years before. Probably, they'd had to relearn how to love each other.

Alan stepped off the sailboat wearing a tan short-sleeved button-down and a pair of slacks. He looked strong and happy, and he lifted Nora into him as they kissed, getting lipstick all over his lips. Nora laughed and tidied him up, but he swatted her away and kissed her again, saying, "Bright red is my color."

Alan drove Nora's car out to The Jessabelle House, where the "re-do" party for Benny's remission was set to begin at four that afternoon. Throughout the drive, Alan and Nora spoke to one another obsessively, telling everything they'd done and everything they'd thought since they'd last seen one another a few days ago. Had anyone overheard them, they'd have thought they were teenagers. As Alan updated her about the state of his tomato plants, Nora sat captivated, thinking, *This is the most interesting man in the world.* That was the nature of love. It altered the chemistry of your mind.

The Jessabelle House was located at the top of the bluffs outside the village of Siasconset. Nora had seen it from a distance numerous times but had never gotten close. Yet as they drove down the driveway, getting closer and closer, the old Victorian seemed illuminated, with a number of ornate details that reminded you that, once upon a time, architects had been the true artists of the world. Alan parked Nora's car alongside several others, then smiled at her and squeezed her hand.

"Oriana said she's already here," Alan said.

"Do you know if Roland and Grant are coming?" Nora asked.

Alan grimaced. "It sounds like they're still keeping their distance. Oriana is sick about it, I'm afraid."

Nora sighed. More than anyone, she understood how fear could hold you back from living your life and from saying everything that needed to be said. She wished she could impart this knowledge to Roland and Grant to tell them they had a limited time on this earth.

"Oriana and Meghan deserve to know their brothers," she said quietly to Alan.

"That they do," Alan said. "And who wouldn't want to know Oriana and Meghan?" He smiled sheepishly as he added, "They're certainly smitten with you. They're always asking me when I'm going to bring you to Martha's Vineyard for keeps."

Nora's eyes became wide as her heart performed a victory dance. This was what she wanted more than anything. Then again, she'd only known Alan for less than a month! *Was any of this rational?*

"I told them I'm letting you take the reins on our relationship," Alan explained.

"So, this is a relationship now, is it?" Nora teased, trying to catch her breath.

"I'd like to call you my girlfriend, yes," Alan said. "Unless that sounds too silly. Then, I'll call you 'the only woman I want to share a bed with.'" His cheeks became crimson with embarrassment, but he maintained eye contact throughout.

Nora leaned across the car and kissed him with her eyes closed. At this moment, she remembered what had happened a few days ago, when she'd told Alan that she'd run into Jeffrey at Marcus' grave. (She never wanted to lie to Alan about anything, not even a lie of omission would do.) Alan had sounded surprised and genuinely happy for her.

"It sounds like you both have unfinished business," he'd said. "And it's good you can face the past together this time, after so long apart." Nora's heart had filled with gladness at that. "I'd love to meet him one day," Alan had said then. "I hope you'll invite me to dinner sometime."

"I'd like that," Nora had said.

Nora and Alan stepped out of the car and were immediately struck with the fluttering conversation coming from the veranda of The Jessabelle House. Music stirred through the air, and a soft breeze swept off the nearby ocean. Alan took Nora's hand and led her to the steps that went up to the veranda, where they paused for a moment to gaze at the beautiful Colemans on high— both the Nantucket and the Martha's Vineyard variety.

"Nora! Alan!" Oriana appeared at the top of the steps and beckoned for them to come up.

Slowly, Nora and Alan walked up the steps, bringing more and more of the party into view. When they reached the top, Oriana swallowed Nora with a hug, then waved toward Alexa, who carried Benny around with her, as though she couldn't possibly let him go. Even since the last time she'd seen him, Benny had grown more hair on his head, and he babbled excitedly to Alan until Alan eventually took him in his arms and walked toward Benny's toy trucks in the corner of the veranda, which Benny wanted to show off.

"Nora, I have several more paintings for you," Alexa said, "if you'd like to feature them at your art store."

"I would love that," Nora said. "Your paintings have created quite a buzz, you know."

"It's true. I heard her name whispered amongst other art dealers I know," Oriana said, her eyebrows raised. "I was like, wait! That's my daughter! She lives in my house!"

"Which is how Mom got me a pretty sweet gallery deal in Brooklyn," Alexa explained timidly.

"That's fantastic!" Nora cried. "Wow. Maybe Alan and I should come to the city to see it."

"It's not like the work I sell at your store," Alexa explained. "It's much darker, made during the time when Benny was very sick. It was a way for me to put that energy somewhere."

"That makes sense," Nora said.

In the distance, a truck began to snake up the driveway. Nora squinted at it to make out the image of Charlie Coleman in the front seat.

"Oh! Wonderful. The last of our guests," Oriana said.

Nora watched as Charlie parked the truck in the driveway, then hurried around to the back to help Marcy out. Jax stepped out of the back, as well, carrying Marcy's crutches. From up on the veranda, Marcy seemed bright and healthy, her skin porcelain, with only the slightest signs of the recent accident.

Charlie carried Marcy up the steps of the porch as everyone called out hello. Marcy waved, pretending to be a princess, her cheeks pink. Charlie then set Marcy up at one of the picnic tables as Jax hurried over to place her crutches near her and kiss her on the cheek. The sight of their love filled Nora's heart.

"Aunt Nora!" Jax stepped away from Marcy to hug Nora, his eyes alight. "I'm glad you made it."

"This is the famous Jax?" Oriana smiled and stuck out her hand. "My name is Oriana. This is my daughter, Alexa."

"Famous?" Jax laughed as he shook their hands. "I don't know about that."

"Our Nora loves you to bits," Oriana explained. "We've heard all about you. And we've been pulling for you and Marcy over on Martha's Vineyard."

Jax glanced back toward Marcy, who nodded in conversation with Charlie. Charlie seemed to sense Nora's gaze, and he turned and raised a hand. Nora returned the wave, feeling mystified. *How was it possible she was at a party with Charlie Coleman? How was it possible so much had changed so quickly?*

"Do you want to meet Marcy?" Jax asked Nora. In his eyes, Nora sensed just how much this meant to him.

Nora nodded and followed after him, walking very slowly as she neared the beautiful young woman. The truth of it was that Marcy had lived, and Marcus had died. But any life was meant to be celebrated. And Marcy still had a whole lot of life to live, just as Nora did.

"Marcy? I want to introduce you to my Aunt Nora," Jax said, his hand on Marcy's shoulder.

Marcy raised her chin and looked at Nora happily. From this close up, Nora could see far more of the girl's scars, and the cast around her leg was very thick. Marcy stuck out her hand to shake Nora's, then said, "It's wonderful to meet you. Jax won't shut up about your garden."

Nora laughed with surprise. "What did he say?"

"He said you have the greenest thumb in the world," Marcy said. "And that it's like an oasis in your backyard."

Nora blushed. "I like to think so."

"Maybe you can show me a thing or two about gardening?" Marcy suggested. "I'm going to be a teacher in about a year, God willing, and I'd really love to have a class garden with my students. I feel like kids these days don't really understand food, how it's grown, and where it comes from, and I would love to give them a sense of how long a seed takes to sprout, how to weed and care for vegetables, and how to prepare little salads from the garden."

Nora's heart opened up at the idea of teaching this young teacher about things so dear to her heart. She imagined her knowledge in the garden spreading to hundreds upon hundreds of Marcy's students over the years, even long after Nora herself was gone.

"Maybe you and your father can come over sometime," Nora said timidly.

"If I remember correctly, you make the very best lemonade," Charlie said, his eyes heavy with memory.

"She does," Jax affirmed. "I can never get enough."

"Sounds like it's a date," Marcy said sweetly.

"But it'll have to be soon," Nora said softly, glancing across the veranda at Alan. "I don't think I'll be in Nantucket long."

"Oh?" Charlie's lips parted with surprise.

"I'm making changes," Nora said, her eyes filling with tears. "And those changes very well might lead me elsewhere, where I can finally start over."

"But you'll still have a garden?" Marcy asked.

Nora laughed and said, "Of course," thinking of the garden that she and Alan would share together in Martha's Vineyard— how it would widen, grow stronger and greener with each passing year. They would experiment with different varieties of vegetables and keep a record of how they'd grown and then weed and laugh together as the Martha's Vineyard sun beat gently down upon them. Oh, her heart just sang at the idea of those beautiful future afternoons filled with love.

Coming Next in the Coleman Series

Pre-order Waves of Time

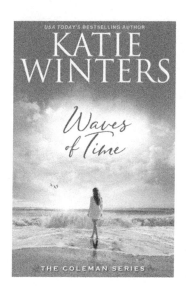

Other Books by Katie Winters

The Vineyard Sunset Series

Secrets of Mackinac Island Series

Sisters of Edgartown Series

A Katama Bay Series

A Mount Desert Island Series

A Nantucket Sunset Series